Aghast, Melissa stood at the restaurant entrance and gaped at the tall stranger who stepped into the line of fire just as she threw Guido's gift back at his messenger.

The go-between seized the opportunity to duck into his flashy black Lincoln and take off like a shot.

With his hand cupped over one eye, the stranger glanced at the retreating car, shifted his attention to the chocolate bonbons strewn over the ground, and then looked at Melissa. If she hadn't felt so awful for nailing him with the candy box, she might have giggled at the completely bamboozled expression on his face. A nice face, a part of her mind noted.

"I'm so sorry. Are you okay?"

His gaze dropped to the chocolates once more, then lifted to her. "Not your particular choice of flavor?"

PAMELA GRIFFIN lives in Texas and divides her time among family, church activities, and writing. She fully gave her life to the Lord in 1988 after a rebellious young adulthood and owes the fact that she's still alive today to an all-loving and forgiving God and a mother who prayed that her wayward daughter would "come home." Pamela's main goal in writing Christian romance is to encourage others through entertaining stories that also heal the wounded spirit.

Please visit Pamela at: www.PamelaGriffin.com

Books by Pamela Griffin

HEARTSONG PRESENTS

HP372—Til We Meet Again
HP420—In the Secret Place
HP446—Angels to Watch Over Me
HP469—Beacon of Truth
HP520—The Flame Within
HP560—Heart Appearances
HP586—A Single Rose
HP617—Run Fast, My Love
HP697—Dear Granny
HP711—A Gentle Fragrance

Don't miss out on any of our super romances. Write to us at the following address for information on our newest releases and club information.

Heartsong Presents Readers' Service
PO Box 721
Uhrichsville, OH 44683

Or visit www.heartsongpresents.com

A Bridge Across the Sea

Pamela Griffin

Heartsong Presents

Thank you to Jill Stengl, Therese Travis, and Adrie Ashford for your invaluable help and constant support as you cheered me along and critiqued chapters in record time. Mom, that goes for you, too. You're incredible. . . .

Dedicated to my Lord and Savior, who guides me along unfamiliar paths and makes a bridge across when there seems no other way.

A note from the Author:
I love to hear from my readers! You may correspond with me by writing:

Pamela Griffin
Author Relations
PO Box 721
Uhrichsville, OH 44683

ISBN 1-59789-384-6

A BRIDGE ACROSS THE SEA

Our mission is to publish and distribute inspirational products offering exceptional value and biblical encouragement to the masses.

PRINTED IN THE U.S.A.

prologue

1928

Peter, have you not heard a word I've spoken? Must I be harsh and reveal to you what we both already know? You ask for reasons why we cannot marry, yet those reasons should be obvious under the circumstances. Mummy would never abide my marriage to a man who is nameless.

Nameless. . .

Nameless. . .

"Excuse me, sir?"

Torn from the distressing memory of his last encounter with Claire, Peter Caldwell turned his head to look at the steward who had come up beside him.

"Yes?"

"Is everything all right?" The boy's eyes lowered to Peter's white knuckles clutching the ship's rail, then seemed to latch onto the cane hooked around his wrist, staring at the walking stick longer than necessary. "Are ye feeling well, sir?"

"Well?" Peter gave a dry chuckle.

He supposed he felt as well as a survivor of the *Titanic* disaster could feel when faced with the reality of sailing across the ocean again. Of course, he'd only been a small lad and remembered next to nothing of that time at sea. Once he'd feverishly worked to escape what little of the horror he did recall; now, ironically, the tragic sinking of sixteen years ago took him to America. He needed to discover what had happened that night so he could bury the vague memories that haunted his days.

Peter collected himself and eyed the lad, who looked only a

few years younger than his own twenty-two. "Yes, thank you. I am well."

"It's only that you look a little green around the gills, sir. Travel on an ocean liner isn't for everyone, and anyone can be affected. Had a bit of the seasickness myself when I worked my first voyage, but it goes away after a spell. Would ye like me to direct you to the ship's physician?"

"No, thank you. Once I partake of some sustenance, I should feel better, I think. There's nothing quite like a good meal to soothe a man's stomach. Even at sea. Or so I've been told."

The steward laughed. "Aye, and this ship has the best gourmet food there is, though just between you and me, mate. . ." He leaned in closer as if to divulge a secret. "My tastes run more toward the Italian variety."

"Italian? I can't say as I've tried that."

"You've never tried Italian food? Spaghetti? Or lasagna?"

Peter's mouth twitched. "To my knowledge, England doesn't contain a wealth of Old Italy. This is actually my first voyage. . . in a long time."

The boy's mouth dropped open. "Incredible. To be so well off a bloke as yourself and not to have indulged in the pleasures of pasta?" He shook his head as if Peter were missing out on something ideal. "Once we dock in Manhattan, you must try Marelli's. It has the best Italian food, I'll wager. Whenever we come to port, I eat there. And the blond waitress who works there? Cute as a button, she is." He winked and jabbed Peter in the ribs as if they were old shipmates.

Ignoring the steward's lack of protocol, Peter wondered how he'd gone from *sir* to *mate* in the span of seconds, but that was often the case. Strangers relaxed and let down their guards around him. He'd been told this was partly due to his dry wit. Not that humor in any form was a bad thing. His mother had said putting people at ease and making them laugh was a gift. . .his mother.

As he dwelt on the image, another woman's features came

to mind. Peter sobered, averting his gaze to the waves rippling beneath him. The steward, obviously sensing the mood change, excused himself and left Peter to stare sightlessly out over the wide, unforgiving ocean.

He only prayed this voyage wasn't a mistake and that he would find the answers for which he'd been searching—both in his mind, since as a boy of seven he'd lost so much dear to him, and with his actions, since he'd purchased the ticket to New York and had given free rein to this burning desire to obtain truth. He had searched for the answers in England before this venture, but not with the present boldness that compelled him to dig deeper now.

It was too late to turn back the hands of time. His only recourse remained to press forward, and that was exactly what he intended to do. No matter the cost to his heart.

one

Peter walked along the piers flanking the Hudson River, impressed by the massive ships docked there. As he shielded his eyes against the late-morning sun's glare and looked to the east, he noted the rigging of one ship in the process of being built. Beyond the docks, the Statue of Liberty emerged from the morning mist, her torch raised in silent hope. Seagulls cried out in mournful song as dockworkers toiled at their duties, and beyond that, the river glimmered as if it held its own secrets. The salty odor of fish permeated the foggy air.

Pulling his gaze away from the wharf, Peter focused on his destination. An old fisherman had given him directions to the simple building that housed a part of his past. The sign above the door read: WHITE STAR LINES LIMITED.

He hesitated before gripping the handle. One step farther through that door and he would forever terminate the possibility of letting go of the past. Buried secrets could cause pain once rocks were uncovered, as his father had warned before Peter left Liverpool. But they could also release him from the nightmare of ignorance that had held him bound for so many years.

A story from his childhood came to mind, and he wondered which would greet him when he opened the door: news of the lady for whom he had yearned, or the merciless tiger that would finish him off for embarking on this foolish quest. He thought of Claire and hardened his resolve to find the answers. Without further hesitation, he opened the door.

Inside, the room stood in disorder. No one occupied the desk piled awry with ledgers, papers, and packing crates.

"Hello?" Peter's greeting brought no answer. He looked

around the room and toward a narrow corridor, also empty. "I say, is anyone about?"

The sound of shuffling shoes on the tiled floor preceded the appearance of an elderly bewhiskered gentleman. His clothes were worn, his shoulders bent, but the welcoming smile on his face seemed genuine. In his gnarled hands, he carried a mop and pail.

"Good morning. We don't get much business this early of a morning. I would think Mr. Fromby'll be here soon though." He set the pail down and went to work cleaning up a brown spill that Peter now saw beside the desk. "Please excuse the disorder. We're a lot more efficient than appearances show, I assure you. Since the White Star Lines Limited was included with the Royal Mail Steam Packet Company last year—unofficially of course—things haven't settled down yet. Lots of shifting around, you understand."

Apparently the gentleman was a talker, something that could work in Peter's favor. "Perhaps you could help me? I'm seeking an old passenger list—sixteen years old, to be exact."

A gleam of interest shone in the old man's blue eyes. "That so? You a reporter?"

"A reporter?"

"Only ship that collected any interest from 1912 was the *Titanic*. I imagine that's the list you're wanting?"

"Yes, that's what I need. And this is for personal reasons. I'm not a reporter."

The man set the mop into the pail. "Well now, I would imagine that list would be in the archives room. I was here in the office that day." He shook his head. "A terrible day it was, too."

"Yes, I can well imagine. Is there any way I could see the list?"

"I'm not authorized to touch the records, or I'd help you, young fellow. You'll need to talk to Mr. Fromby. The White Star created a raw list for the hearings, both here and in Britain. That where you're from? You have the accent."

"Yes, near London, actually."

"Thought so. Don't get many Britishers in this office. I'm Roger, by the way. You writing a book?"

Peter was exhausted; leisurely chat held no appeal. The dream had revisited his mind last night, likely brought on by his quest, and he had slept little. "When do you expect Mr. Fromby?"

"Hard to tell with him. On Mondays, he usually doesn't show up 'til after lunchtime. Visits the piers and such in the morning. You won't get past his secretary though, and who knows where she is." He tapped his skull with a forefinger. "She's a bit touched in the head; don't trust nobody, which is wise in Manhattan, what with all the crime, I suppose. But she carries it to the extreme."

"Perhaps I'll check back later, regardless." Peter had braved his qualms and sailed across an entire ocean to reach his goal; a cagey secretary wouldn't prevent him from reaching it.

"You could always try, that's a fact. You find a place to stay?"

"Yes, actually. I have a room at the Waldorf-Astoria."

"A ritzy place, but then you look as if you can afford the extras." Roger's offhand comment didn't seem rude when matched with his wide grin; Peter had the feeling he was always one to speak his mind, no matter the occasion.

"Say. . ." His eyes lit up. "I might be able to help some at that. I know the names and locales of a few survivors who settled down in or around the city. People I've come to know over the years. I may be getting on in years, but my memory's still sharp as a tack." He grinned. "I could give the information to you, if you want to contact them for that book you're writing. Though I can't give you Mr. Ismay's address; not long after he resigned as president of the White Star line, a year after the *Titanic* sank, he left the public eye. People didn't take too kindly to him surviving when the ship's own captain went down."

"I would appreciate any help you can give me." Uncomfortable about sharing his personal history with strangers and certain that if he did, the whole of New York City would know of it by nightfall, Peter didn't correct Roger's assumption that he was writing a book.

Hours later, armed with Roger's list, Peter hailed a cab that deposited him near Marelli's. The morning had been a disappointment. The one locale Peter had tried, when he finally found the place, yielded no results; the owners weren't home. Perhaps taking the ship steward's recommendation to sample an Italian meal might improve the afternoon's outlook.

As Peter approached the door, a man sped out of it.

"And you can take this back where it came from, too!" a woman yelled.

Startled, Peter swung his attention toward the restaurant door just as a square box came hurtling his way and struck him in the eye.

❧

Aghast, Melissa stood at the restaurant entrance and gaped at the tall stranger who stepped into the line of fire just as she threw Guido's gift back at his messenger. The go-between seized the opportunity to duck into his flashy black Lincoln and take off like a shot.

With his hand cupped over one eye, the stranger glanced at the retreating car, shifted his attention to the chocolate bonbons strewn over the ground, and then looked at Melissa. If she hadn't felt so awful for nailing him with the candy box, she might have giggled at the completely bamboozled expression on his face. A nice face, a part of her mind noted.

"I'm so sorry. Are you okay?"

His gaze dropped to the chocolates once more, then lifted to her. "Not your particular choice of flavor?"

Totally unexpected, the wry comment delivered in a crisp British accent made her eyes widen in incredulity. She gave a light laugh. In an instant, she felt at ease with this man, which then slowly put her on her guard. Melissa's trust had never been easily won by any man, and she suspected guilt prodded her to relax her defenses now. Despite this, she moved closer.

"Not my particular choice of suitor, either. Is it bad? Your eye, I mean?"

He pulled his hand away to let her see, and she winced. The corner of the box had caught him beneath his left eyebrow. On top of the bruised skin, a beaded line of red had appeared.

"Come inside and let me tend to that," she offered. "It's the least I can do after walloping you."

"I would appreciate it. I was intending to visit in any case. I was told I must sample the food here."

"Yes, it is good. But then, I'm biased in that regard."

She smiled and retraced her steps, then stopped when she noticed he wasn't following, and looked over her shoulder. He had stooped low, putting his weight on his cane, to scrape up the chocolates from the sidewalk and drop them back into the box.

"Oh, no. Please. You don't have to do that. Really, I feel bad enough as it is. I'll clean it up after we get you inside."

"Already finished," he said, collecting another handful and tossing them into the container. He rose with some difficulty and moved closer; it was then she noticed his slight limp and how he relied on the black cane to walk. He handed her the box. She took it, suddenly awash with shyness. Now that she wasn't focused on the incident or his wound, she couldn't help but notice how clear and bright his eyes were. And blue. As blue as the late-summer sky and lighter than her own. He appeared much younger than she'd first thought, too young to need a cane. She suspected he was no more than a couple of years older than she.

"Well. . ." Never at a loss for words, she suddenly couldn't find a one of them.

He stuck out his right hand. "Peter Caldwell, at your service."

"Melissa Reynolds," she said in a quick exhalation of air, still flustered. She gathered her wits and took his hand. . .strangely she found she didn't want to let go. Her heart stood still. His eyes flickered, and she broke contact, dropping her hand to her side.

What was she doing, acting all googly-eyed like some silly flapper—and to a complete stranger, yet? If her cousins saw, she would never hear the end of it.

"Your eye's getting worse every second we stand out here," she said to hide the rush of feeling that had surged through her at the strange connection she'd felt with him. "Come along, and I'll get you some ice. We don't have steaks here."

"Ice is preferable. I never was partial to raw meat."

At his careless quip, she again glanced at him, trying to figure him out, then gave a slight shake of her head and led the way inside. Relieved this was a slow time of the day—or she would never have gone off like a hothead and made a spectacle of herself earlier—she seated him at a table inside the empty restaurant.

"Just wait here, and I'll be right back." She handed him a menu from a nearby table. "And please, choose whatever you'd like. Your meal's on me."

"I could never dream of allowing such a thing."

"It would make me feel better, considering."

"It truly isn't necessary. I'm well aware that you didn't intend to wallop me—isn't that how you Americans say it?" His eyes teased, and she caught a breath.

"Well, yes, but you don't understand. My aunt Maria and uncle Tony own this restaurant, and I know they would also insist your meal be on the house. So no more arguments. *Capisci?*"

Before he could offer further objections, she headed to the kitchen to chip ice off one of the blocks in the walk-in freezer. Aunt Maria stood near the stove, stirring a huge vat of fragrant sauce. Spanish in heritage, she only grew more beautiful with each passing year. That she married an Italian and could cook better than any of Tony's sisters was the ongoing joke in the Marelli family.

Melissa felt her aunt watching her quick actions as she ducked into the freezer. Aunt Maria's eyebrows arched in curiosity when Melissa exited.

"For a customer," she explained, not yet willing to admit her embarrassing mistake. She felt a betraying flush swamp her face, which in retrospect was welcome after her mission in the freezer.

"*Mi niña*, I sense there is something you're not telling me."

Aunt Maria's use of her girlhood nickname made Melissa feel little more than a child, and as she did then, Melissa found herself defending her actions now.

"I didn't mean to hurt anyone."

"Oh, dear." Aunt Maria stopped stirring. "What have you done?"

"I, um, accidentally bashed a guy with the candy box I was throwing at one of Guido's henchmen."

The name of Vittorio's nephew made her aunt gasp. Alarm filled her dark eyes. "Oh, no. You must be careful. You do not want to get on that man's bad side. He is very dangerous."

"I know that." Melissa smiled to relieve her aunt's fears. "But I don't want to go out with him either, so how do you suggest I get the message across to him? A simple no didn't work—all ten times I tried it. Today was the third time he sent one of his thugs over with flowers or candy." She looked down at the melting ice in the cup. "I need to get back out there. Poor guy. He's going to have quite a shiner."

"Well, be sure and let him know whatever he wants is on the house."

"I already have," Melissa said with a smile and returned to the table.

Peter had removed his felt hat, which sat in the chair beside him, and Melissa could now see his hair was straight and dark blond. He read a piece of paper he held in both hands. When he lifted his gaze, stunned awareness filled his eyes, though he politely stood as she approached.

She waved him back down. "Is everything all right?"

"Your aunt Maria, she is Maria Marelli? A survivor of the *Titanic* disaster?"

A jolt of surprise shot through Melissa, transporting her back through time. She cleared her throat, glanced at the paper clutched in his hand, then looked back into his eyes. "Why do you wish to know?"

"Because she might be able to help me locate my family."

two

Peter stared at the lovely woman before him. Shock clouded her cornflower blue eyes, and she shook her head of short blond curls, as though she struggled to follow his words. She gripped the back of a chair, as if she might pass out.

"Your family was on the *Titanic?*" she asked through stiff lips.

"Not those for whom I'm looking, no. But my mother and I were both passengers."

At this, she sat down with a swift thump. "You were on the *Titanic?*"

Peter wondered at her inability to fathom his words, when realization struck. "You were on the *Titanic* as well." It was a statement, not a question; her actions made it clear.

With a dull nod, she closed her eyes. "I celebrated my fifth birthday there." Her gaze grew unfocused as the seconds elapsed and she slipped into another time. "Such a party it was, too; I may have been very young, but I remember. My mother even secured a steward to play the part of a clown to entertain us, and the ship's musicians played nearby, in the adjoining room. A kind woman arrived late to the party, a passenger I wanted to be there, and she gave me a blanket for my new doll."

Her vague words opened a mist-shrouded memory inside Peter, and his eyes opened wider. "There was a waiter, a clumsy fellow. He knocked into the table and. . .something fell." He pulled his brows together in an effort to remember.

Her attention swung back to him. "The punch glasses," she said as if dazed. "He fell against a chair and grabbed the tablecloth. All the crystal went crashing to the floor. He was funnier than the clown." A quiet giggle escaped. "Mama was livid. She complained to the head steward that she suspected the man was inebriated."

"And the musicians began playing louder to cover her screeching—"

"Then the captain's mate came in to see what all the ruckus was about—"

"And she said if it were her ship, she'd make them all walk the plank."

Peter and Melissa stared at one another in wonder, each softly smiling as the tenuous bond drew them together.

"I liked stories of pirates, so perhaps that's why I remembered," Peter explained.

"Mama invited all the first- and second-class passengers' children to the Café Parisian for my party. . .and you were there." She breathed the last words in awe, then blinked as if suddenly bashful, her gaze dropping to the cup she held. "Oh, dear. Your eye." Quickly, she poured ice into a napkin and bunched it up. She lifted the compress to his head but hesitated before contact could be made. Sensing her discomfiture, Peter held out his hand, and she gave the ice to him.

"Do you remember anything else about your time on the ship?" He pressed the cloth over his eye. The extreme cold burned his skin, but he kept the frozen napkin in place.

"Some things. Not a lot."

"What about that last night? Do you remember any of it?"

A haunted look swam through her eyes. "How could I forget?" she said simply.

He nodded and glanced at his cane propped against the table. "I bear a continual reminder; that night crippled me for life. Unfortunately, it crippled my memory, as well."

Her expression softened in sympathy. "I suffered no physical injuries, only emotional ones—as I'm sure every other survivor did. I still suffer from nightmares."

At the word *nightmare*, Peter tensed, thinking of his own. The one with his mother that always ended at the same spot.

"I remember very little of that night, though some events, like your birthday party, are now clear to me. However, your party only became vivid after you spoke of it. Perhaps that's the key to unlocking the rest of what happened. Finding those who will speak of the events to spur the recollections."

"You *want* to remember?"

He nodded. "My mother died that night, and my family couldn't be found when we docked. It's one of the reasons I'm here."

Before she could respond, a dark-haired woman strode toward them, and Peter stood to his feet. Her hair was secured in a braid around her head reminiscent of an old-fashioned Mediterranean style. Peter guessed her to be in her mid-thirties, though her olive skin was still as fresh as dew and her cheeks bloomed with healthy pink.

"Missy, I wondered what was keeping you from giving me the new order." The words were delivered blithely in a melodic Spanish accent, and she then nodded to Peter with a smile. "You must forgive my niece; her aim has never been good. Please, sit down."

Peter looked back and forth between the women, amazed. While Melissa was as fair as a Scandinavian princess, her aunt was as dark as a Spanish *condesa*.

Peter focused his attention on the older woman and offered his hand in greeting. "Mrs. Marelli, allow me to introduce myself. I am Peter Caldwell, recently arrived from Great Britain. Your name was given to me from a worker at the White Star Lines Limited as one of those who survived the tragedy on the *Titanic*."

Maria's eyes flashed wide in surprise, but she gave a short nod.

"I'm trying to locate anyone who was a passenger and might have known my mother or been acquainted with her on the ship." From his coat pocket, he withdrew a bound linen handkerchief and carefully unfolded it to show a gold oval locket resting within its snowy folds, one of two heirlooms he'd brought with him from England. He opened it to reveal a set of pictures, one on each side. Both were badly water damaged, but by some odd act of providence, the face of the woman wasn't harmed. Seawater had obliterated the other face.

"My mother put this around my neck that final night." Peter didn't know that speaking the words after so many years would produce within him such a sudden fount of emotion, and he cleared his throat before going on. "Shortly afterward, she left our cabin. I never saw her again."

Sympathy clouded Maria's brow. "I'm sorry for your loss." She took the locket and studied the picture for several seconds, then handed it back with an apologetic shake of her head. "She doesn't look familiar. But it has been so long, and I spent most of my time taking care of Missy, you understand. I was her niñera—her nanny."

His curiosity must have been evident.

"Aunt Maria and I aren't related by blood but through marriage," Melissa explained. "My mother married her brother when I was three, and Maria took care of me."

"Ah, I see." Still, he wondered that Maria should have taken on the role of servant to her brother's child. Perhaps in America, such protocol wasn't considered unusual.

Maria fondly smiled at the younger woman. "I think of Missy as a daughter; I always have." She looked at Peter. "Have you been in America long?"

"Only since yesterday when the ship docked."

"And you have found a good place to stay?"

Peter had a feeling that, like his adoptive mother, this woman would open her home to him and any other stranger in need. "Thank you, yes. I'm staying at the Waldorf-Astoria, though I've been out since early this morning on my quest. I was told on the ship I must try Italian food. Your restaurant was recommended to me."

Her brows sailed up at his mention of one of the most

exclusive hotels in the city. "Since this morning, you have been searching? And here it is past noon. I assume from your words you have not eaten today?" She threw her hands up, and a stream of Spanish burst from her lips. Peter had the feeling he was being chided for not taking care of himself. "So, you never have had Italian food, Peter Caldwell? Then I must make you one of the best meals we have to offer."

"Please, don't go to any trouble on my account." He recalled what the steward on the boat had said. "A plate of spaghetti sounds like a splendid idea."

"*Sí, sí.* You shall have the spaghetti and more. Missy, keep our customer happy while I prepare his meal."

Both women grinned at Peter, and Maria hurried away.

"You might as well give up," Melissa said. "She is a force to be reckoned with when she's made up her mind."

"I don't want to put her out."

She gave a light laugh. "This is a restaurant, Peter! It's our job to serve you." She blushed. "I hope you don't mind if I call you Peter. I mean, since you were at my birthday party, I feel as if I know you."

"I would consider it an honor. And may I call you Missy? Or would you prefer Melissa?"

"Well, normally I only allow Maria to call me that since it sounds so babyish. But I guess I don't mind if you do, too."

"I rather like it." And he did. The nickname was as pert and delightful as the bearer; she was more than delightful actually. Missy had a fresh, delicate beauty about her china-doll-like features, and he felt as if he could stare into her pretty eyes all day. Realizing where his mind was taking him, he looked down at the paper in his hands, feeling a twinge of guilt. Claire had told him she couldn't marry him and why, but the only reason he'd journeyed to America on this search was to discover his heritage. He was already well on the road to finding answers and hoped soon the mystery of his past would no longer present a problem.

"The other names on the list," Missy said, breaking into his thoughts. "May I see them?"

"Of course." Peter handed the paper over and watched her expression, but no recognition lit her features.

"I was very young," she apologized, handing the list back. "Do you know your way around New York? Do you have a map of the area?"

"No, though I suppose I should purchase one. Especially to find this third place." He briefly looked at the paper to read the locale. "Coney Island. Do you know of it? Is this island far off the coast?"

She giggled, and he found he liked the sound. It didn't seem silly, flirtatious, or even childish; rather, her laugh was light and buoyant.

"It's a famous amusement park, a New Yorker's playground," she said. "You really don't know our city well if you've never heard of Coney Island, do you?"

"This is my first visit to America. I've lived my entire life in England, though I've traveled with my family to other parts of Great Britain."

Her brow wrinkled in puzzlement. "You said you couldn't find your family."

"My adoptive family. The truth is. . ." He hesitated, wondering why he found it easy to share matters with her that he'd guarded from others, even close friends, for years. Perhaps it had something to do with the fact that they'd both been passengers on the ill-fated ship.

"Yes, Peter?"

He saw only kindness in her eyes.

"The truth is, I don't know my given surname. That night wiped out a great deal of my memory, and the name which I'd associated with my mother the few times I heard her addressed by it wasn't on the ship's manifest, according to my adoptive father. I was too young to look at the time, of course."

She leaned forward, placing her fingertips against his sleeve in an unconscious gesture. "Oh, Peter. How awful for you!" She held his gaze a moment, then looked down at his sleeve as if just aware she'd touched him. Moving her hand away, she stared at the table, clearly embarrassed by her action.

Touched by her gesture, Peter wanted to relieve any qualms she might have concerning him and softened his voice a degree. "I'm not certain what I'm hoping to find or even if I'll find anything. So many years have elapsed. This entire venture might prove fruitless, but I won't know if I don't try."

She gave an encouraging smile and nod.

"Somehow, I know if I find any answers, they will be here, in America. In New York to be precise. I do remember. . ." He hesitated. "She told me I would meet my father in New York City."

"He didn't come to the dock to collect you when the *Carpathia* pulled in?"

"If he did, I wouldn't know it. I was in the infirmary, being treated for frostbite. But even if he had been in the same room with me, I wouldn't have recognized his face. He was never a part of my life. We were sailing to America to see him. And there's a good possibility. . ." Again he hesitated, uncertain why he was telling all this to a stranger. Yet speaking with Missy didn't feel like addressing a stranger. Due to the connection they shared, she seemed more than that. "There's a possibility that my mother never married. I need to know, to discover the truth. No matter what it leads to."

To Missy's credit, she didn't show one iota of shock, nor did she draw away in doubt the way Claire had when she'd learned of Peter's secret. Missy remained quiet a moment, her attention dropping to the list he held open in his hands. "And you feel that one of those six people might hold the key?"

"I can only hope so. Though what the key is, I don't know. Perhaps speaking with others will bring back the same clarity of memory you've given me and trigger a memory which will in turn, lead me to my family or at least the knowledge of one." He shrugged. "It's a bit farfetched, I know. But I have nothing else to go by. I haven't any other method with which to start my search."

"I think if I were in your position, I'd do the same." Her expression became serious. . . ." This time she was the one to hesitate. "Peter, I'd like to help you, if you'll let me."

"Help me?" Stunned curiosity made him straighten in his chair.

"You don't know your way around the city. I know where most of the places are on that list—or at least how to get to them."

"I wouldn't wish to take advantage of your time."

"You wouldn't be. Besides, I offered." She gave a quirk of a smile. "This is a slow time of year for the restaurant. My uncle Tony's been suffering from arthritis in his elbow, and many of our patrons come only to hear him play the violin. He is quite the virtuoso. At this point, he's not playing, so that means business isn't as steady as usual; besides, our busiest hours are in the evenings, and as you can clearly see. . . ." She waved a hand around the empty restaurant. "We aren't exactly at standing room only."

"But you know nothing about me except what I've told you." Were all American women so trusting of unknown foreign men?

"I know enough to sense you're not dangerous. Any man who offers a witty comeback after having been mistakenly knocked in the eye with a flying candy box from an irate blond can't be all that bad." She grinned. "And if you still think I'm a nut for offering to tag along with you, then let me reassure you here and now that I can take care of myself. Uncle Tony gave me a few boxing lessons when I was younger."

"You're joshing me."

"No, but then you don't know my uncle Tony." She giggled.

Her laughter was contagious, and he joined in then winced as a jolt of pain shot through his eye.

Her expression turned sympathetic. "Besides, you'll be doing me a favor. I have a personal reason I'd like to remain absent from the restaurant for a while."

"The man with the candy?" Peter asked.

"Almost." She grimaced. "He's just the associate. It's his boss I want to keep my distance from."

Peter wondered about the sudden hard glint in her eyes, but she then turned them on him and smiled again. "So what do you say, Peter, ole pal. Mind if I hook up with you on your hunt?"

"Ole pal?" He hitched up his eyebrows, and she chuckled.

"Well, we're *almost* kin, aren't we? The children of the *Titanic*? That has to count for something."

He studied her again, thinking what a pretty girl she was. As he dwelt on their conversation, his words grew curious. "On the voyage to America, a steward recommended this restaurant to me. At the White Star offices, a worker offered me the list of names, and your aunt's was one of six there."

"See? It must be fate that brought us together," Missy teased.

"Fate? Or a higher power?"

She ran her fingertip along the squares in the checked tablecloth before looking at him again. "Do you believe God ordains the paths of those here on earth? Or do you believe it's all left up to chance?"

He grew serious. "I was raised to believe and serve the Lord, but sometimes the answers to such questions are beyond my comprehension."

She gave a weak smile and nod. "That's about the size of it. We don't really know, do we, Peter? But for whatever purpose, destiny seems to have brought you here to us."

Her words alerted a hidden memory, but it faded into the mists of his mind before he could get a good grip on it.

"Peter? Are you okay?" She leaned forward.

He nodded, waving off her concern. "Just a thought. Nothing more."

"A thought?"

He looked into her curious eyes and smiled. "I suppose I cannot fight what is meant to be. If you'd like to come along on my hunt, I could certainly use a guide."

Her radiant smile made even the knock in the eye seem worthwhile.

three

Melissa hurried through her toiletries at record speed the following morning. A tap sounded at her open door, and she turned to see.

Aunt Maria walked into her bedroom, her arms full of towels. "Are you sure about this, Missy?"

"You mean, will I be safe?" Melissa chuckled. "The man's a bona fide gentleman. Did you notice how he stood when each of us entered the restaurant? I've never seen a guy do that except in reel-to-reels at the picture show."

Her aunt gave a slight nod.

"And did you notice the tender way he spoke of his mother? He has a kind heart. Not something you find often in the men of New York City. At least not the men I know." Peter's mention of God had also surprised her, and that he would speak of his faith so freely. She, too, believed in God, but wasn't convinced of His guidance in people's lives, due in part to her own experiences.

"Exactly." Her aunt moved forward, breaking into Melissa's thoughts. "That is what I mean. Are you certain you're not using this only as an excuse to escape your problems regarding Guido?"

Melissa shrugged. "What if I am? Can you blame me?"

"No." Maria's expression softened. "But neither do I wish for you to mistake convenience for anything other than it is."

Melissa laughed in disbelief. "Aunt Maria, I'm going to be Peter's guide for a few days, probably no more than a week. The way you talk, you'd think I was planning my wedding list."

"Just be careful, *mi niña*. I have never known you to offer friendship to a man so quickly." Maria gave her a one-armed hug. "I trust you to listen to your head in this matter and not your heart."

"This, coming from you?" Melissa shook her head. "You're the one who's always prodded me to search for love."

"To be open to it, not to go running after it. It will come when it is time."

Melissa gave a confused shake of her head, looking down at her dresser. "And I told you, Aunt Maria, you have nothing to fear. I just want to help him. Call it an act of charity, helping a fellow survivor. It feels right, somehow."

"Charity? Ah." Maria didn't sound convinced. "Just be careful, that is all I'm asking." She left the room and Melissa to her thoughts.

Melissa pondered the quiet warning. "Still, there is something about him," she said softly to herself.

Firming her lips into a tight line, she fluffed her curls with a brush. Perhaps the desire to aid Peter in his quest did stem from more than just the need to escape Guido's unwanted attentions, or her desire to assist a fellow survivor. But love? Impossible. She had only just met the man, after all. Helping Peter to discover the secrets that went down with the *Titanic* and could lead him to his unknown family might also help her to release her own phantoms of the past, especially those revolving around her mother.

Blissfully ignorant of the world's intrigues and cruelties, Melissa had drifted in her make-believe fantasy world with her niñera always by her side until that last night on *Titanic*. Melissa's innocent eyes had been forced open to harsh truths. Afterward, life swirled into a maelstrom of change, though the treatment she'd endured from one individual remained hopelessly the same.

An unbidden memory of her mother's tinkling laughter and a man's quiet voice outside Melissa's bedroom cabin door rushed to her, and she thumped the brush hard on the dresser. She winced, hoping the wooden handle hadn't scarred the fine oak.

"Missy." Her aunt's voice came from the corridor. "He is here."

Melissa positioned her matching blue hat atop her head at a jaunty angle, stuck the hatpin through the fabric, and grabbed her handbag. She hurried through the corridor leading to the spicy-aroma-filled kitchen, gave a quick nod to her cousin, Cecily, and hurried on into the restaurant, the rapid clicking of her pumps heralding her arrival.

Peter rose from his chair upon sight of her, and she noted the spark of appreciation in his eyes. Usually, she paid little interest to men's favorable attention to her appearance; this morning his notice felt welcomed.

"Hello. So, where should we start?" she cheerily greeted him. A thought struck. "Have you had anything to eat yet?"

"Your aunt's spaghetti and lasagna, while I enjoyed them, do not associate in my mind as breakfast food."

She giggled. "Silly. We do eat other foods here besides pasta. Well, not much, but some. If you're hungry, I noticed Cecily making eggs and bacon. I'm sure she wouldn't mind me begging off a platter."

"Cecily?"

"My uncle Tony's daughter. A cousin."

"If you're sure she won't mind, that would be splendid. I forewent the morning meal."

"I thought so," Melissa playfully chided. "While I understand your eagerness to start this day's activities, you really shouldn't skip eating to do so, Peter. I'll be right back." She hurried to the kitchen and soon returned, bearing a fragrant platter of food and a cup of coffee.

"Your eye looks somewhat better today." She set the plate on the table in front of him. At least the bruise wasn't as dark.

He smiled his thanks, and she noted how he closed his eyes and bowed his head before he took up his fork and began cutting into his egg. She slipped into the chair across from him and smiled as she watched him eat. He really was quite handsome, and he had such a penchant for manners.

He looked up at her. "Would you care for some?"

"Hm? No, I ate earlier."

"Ah." An uneasy smile lifted his lips as he gave a brief nod, then looked down at his food again. Once more he cut a piece of the fluffy egg and raised the fork to his mouth. His eyes lifted to hers and found her still watching.

"I'm sorry. I'm making you nervous, aren't I?" Melissa shifted position in her chair. "It's just that I find myself wondering what you looked like then. I'm trying to place your face at my birthday party."

"Well, I can satisfy your curiosity on that regard. I had very light hair—almost white if you can believe that—and I usually wore an old cap over it. I was skinny; often got myself into mischief."

"You know. . ." A sly smile spread across her face. "I was thinking about the party last night, and I remembered the waiter who knocked over the punch glasses argued that he tripped on something. Later, I found a marble by the wall. Only a few boys came to the party; the rest were girls."

Peter's face reddened as he took a sip of black coffee. "I did carry marbles in my pocket as a lad, but if the one you found was mine, I have no recollection of how it went missing."

Their gazes met, and slow smiles spread across their faces, turning to shared laughter.

"No recollection?" She lifted her brows.

"All right, perhaps there was a hole in my pocket. But no, I truly don't remember. And that's the problem in its entirety. I don't remember."

The words came lightly, his smile growing only a trifle melancholy, but they left an apparent change in the atmosphere. His plight touched Melissa's heart, and she no longer wished to tease him.

"We'll find your answers, Peter. Somehow, we will."

He gave a slight nod, gratitude filling his eyes. "Hearing

you say it, I can almost believe it."

As she continued to stare at him, Melissa's heart twisted, and the impulse to take his hand in hers grew strong. Instead, she excused herself and rose from the table. While he finished his meal, she arranged for their cab.

❧

The first person on Peter's list, according to the address, worked at Macy's Department Store. Peter and Missy stood on the sidewalk and gazed up at the monstrous building that occupied the entire block of Seventh Avenue on the west, Broadway on the east, Thirty-fourth Street on the south, and Thirty-fifth Street on the north. One entire wall of plate glass, the width of a parlor, gave Peter a glimpse of mannequins on elaborate display, draped in the latest evening gowns.

"I love to window shop," Missy said to Peter as they walked under a canopy and toward the glass doors. "I've heard Macy's is the largest department store in the entire world."

Peter could believe it. "It's not Buckingham Palace, but it does come close."

Missy laughed. "There are dozens more like it throughout the city. Saks Fifth Avenue, which is in that direction. . ." Missy motioned across the street. "Altman's, and others."

A man in uniform held the door open and greeted them with a reserved smile. Peter blinked as he took in his first view of Macy's.

In one sweeping glance, he noticed scores of people who busied themselves in every corner of the store. Fashionable shopgirls waited on customers. Male clerks in dark, dignified suits walked the aisles. Everywhere Peter looked, items glittered and gleamed and filled racks and shelves. But the opulence of the store was what caused a moment's shock.

"My word," Peter said, shaking his head.

" 'Goods suitable for the millionaire, at prices in reach of the millions,' " a mustachioed man suddenly said, materializing at their elbows. "That was Rowland Macy's slogan, founder of

Macy's. Now, sir, madam, how may I be of assistance to you this morning?"

"We would like to see ladies' shoes, please," Missy said before Peter could correct the man's assumption that they were married.

He gave them directions, and after a great deal of negotiating the crowded aisles, they approached a plush area lined with women's shoes in a range of colors and styles. A short, bespectacled man approached, his smile as polished as his surroundings. "Good morning. How may I be of service to you?"

"Good morning. We're looking for Mr. Frederick Delaney."

A glint of suspicion entered the clerk's eyes. "That's me."

"Splendid. Mr. Delaney, as a fellow survivor of the *Titanic,* I'm trying to find out any information you might have regarding this woman." Peter withdrew the locket from his coat, but the man darted a glance over his shoulder, as though afraid of discovery.

"Please. If Mr. Hobbs catches me not doing my job, I could get fired."

Missy picked up a navy pump. "I'd like to try this one on, if I may. Size 5."

"Of course, madam." He took the shoe and hurried beyond a drape covering the wall.

Peter curiously eyed Missy, and she shrugged. "If he's doing his work, he might be more inclined to listen."

He smiled in silent agreement. Mr. Delaney returned and took a place on the seat opposite the one Missy had taken. He slipped off her shoe, taking clinical hold of her ankle. His actions revealed a glimpse of her silk-stocking-clad leg. Peter looked at her shapely calf a moment before forcing his attention to a table of footwear, then to the locket in his hand. He opened it and held it suspended from the chain, lowering it in front of the clerk's face.

"Please, sir."

"There were more than two thousand passengers on that ship," the man argued. "I couldn't possibly remember. It's been sixteen years. And if she was in third class, I wouldn't have known her anyway."

"Please. I have reason to believe she was in first or second class." He looked at Missy, remembering his presence at her birthday party. "All I'm asking you to do is look. She. . .she was my mother. She went by the name of Franklin."

The man released a soft breath, then took the locket. "A lovely woman." He stared a moment more. "I don't recall her face. Sorry."

With a dejected nod, Peter closed the locket, slipping it back into his pocket.

"It's not that I don't care." Mr. Delaney's eyes grew sad. "Isidor Straus once owned this department store. After both he and his wife drowned that night, Isidor's brother and later his sons took over. I lost my business shortly after the sinking due to a bad investment, and I never could stop thinking about how it could have been me in Mr. Straus's place. Seeking a position here was my way of giving silent support to those men who lost their lives, to the families of those men. I could have been one of them, you see. But I jumped off before *Titanic* had taken on too much water, and I managed to swim to a boat. One of the very few who did." Tears rimmed his eyes, and Peter sensed the guilt that lay beneath the soft-spoken words. "I could have been one of them."

"Thank you, Mr. Delaney." Peter's own words came quietly. "I understand it's difficult for you to speak of this; I appreciate your time."

The man nodded, slipping the pump off of Missy's foot. "You didn't really want this, did you?"

A sheepish expression crossed her face.

"I didn't think so." Mr. Delaney smiled in a fatherly way, then grew alert, shifting his gaze to Peter. "You said 'fellow survivor' earlier. You were on the *Titanic*?"

Peter looked toward Missy. "Both of us were."

The man swung his surprised focus to Missy again, and she gravely nodded.

"My, my." Mr. Delaney sat back, eyeing them both. "It's a privilege to know two of the children who came through that horrible night, and to know you are alive and well. I helped to load the boats after the chaos began." He pulled out his handkerchief and blotted his eyes, his spectacles inching upward. "Have you visited the memorials?"

"Not as yet," Peter said. "But I plan to. I only arrived from England two days ago."

"You came all the way to America for this? My, my." Mr. Delaney shook his head in wonder. "Listen. I'll tell you what I *can* do. Leave a way that I can reach you, and if I remember anything, I'll be sure to contact you."

"I have a room at the Waldorf-Astoria." Peter reached for his fountain pen and pulled out a small tablet of paper he'd bought for his investigation. "You can reach me here." He scribbled off his name and room number, handing it to Mr. Delaney.

"Caldwell." The man's brows furrowed. "That name. It's very familiar."

"My adoptive mother and father were also on the Titanic." Peter watched the man carefully, not failing to notice Missy's sharp glance in his direction. "Lord Caldwell, he was a viscount at the time of the sinking."

"Oh, yes? I seem to remember the name, but beyond that. . ." He shrugged. "I *am* sorry."

"I appreciate your time." Peter took hold of Missy's elbow and guided her back to the aisle. She seemed pensive, and he wondered what was going through her mind now.

❧

Once back out on the sidewalk, Melissa studied the list.

"Where to next?" Peter asked.

"I recognize one other local address we could try. The others are going to take some time to reach. One is on Long Island; another at Coney Island. I suggest we tackle each of those on separate days. This street," she pointed to an address, "isn't far from here. We could try there next."

"That sounds like a good plan. May I ask a question?"

"Of course."

"How are you so knowledgeable when it comes to determining the locale of addresses on sight?"

She chuckled. "I had a horrible habit of getting lost when I was a child; my uncle Tony made me memorize street names, and some of the addresses are familiar to me because they're places I've been. Macy's for instance," she motioned to the building they'd just left. "Though I'll admit, anything not local will be harder to find; I'm not sure how good a guide I'll be then."

"That's all right. You're good company."

"Thanks. So are you." They shared a smile, then looked ahead again so as not to bump into other pedestrians. "Actually, Peter, you really should take a tour of the city while you're here. I know of some great spots that might interest you."

He nodded. "I could do that."

"Okay, my turn for asking a question."

He chuckled. "Turnabout seems only fair play."

"When you said you were adopted, I assumed you lived in an orphanage after the disaster. But what you told Mr. Delaney, about your adoptive parents being on the *Titanic*— that stunned me. Did you know them? Were they friends of your mother's?"

"No. If they had been, I'd have all the answers I need."

"Of course. I wasn't thinking." Melissa felt stupid for not realizing that.

"No, it's all right." His reassuring tone made her feel not quite so dumb. "My adoptive father, who was then no more than a stranger to me, buckled his life belt around me as well and jumped with me into the water that night. I don't remember any of it, only bits and pieces. I was told about it."

"Oh." She hesitated. "And his wife?"

"She made it to one of the lifeboats before the ship went down. They weren't married then—only childhood sweethearts who'd reunited on the *Titanic*. She lost her father that night, and Lawrence and Annabelle married days after the ship docked. Later they adopted me when no one came to claim me."

Melissa stopped walking suddenly.

"Missy?"

Alarm riddled his voice, but she could barely fathom it. "Annabelle?" She turned wide eyes to him. "Your mother's name is Annabelle?" Her gaze flicked to the side and widened further upon sight of a familiar black Lincoln slowly traveling along the street toward them. All thoughts of the past flew from her mind as she grabbed his free hand. "Come on! We've got to get out of here."

"What? Why?"

"I can't explain now. Just—come on!"

Although crippled, Peter did a remarkable job of keeping up with her. Still, with his limp and her high heels, they weren't fast enough, and dodging the crowds proved difficult. A number of pedestrians sharing the sidewalk aired angry retorts when the two jostled them as they ran past.

"So sorry." Melissa heard Peter call to those with whom they'd had a close skirmish. "Excuse us, please."

Rounding the corner, Melissa dove into the nearest shop, jerking Peter along with her. She halted abruptly and turned, but the force of her unexpected actions toppled Peter into her. To keep from falling, both grabbed each other at their waists in an instinctive gesture. They managed to find their balance, though Melissa's heart went off kilter. She forgot to breathe as, only inches away, Peter's startled blue eyes locked with hers.

four

"Oh."

Missy's soft gasp broke Peter from the enticing harbor of her eyes, reeling him back to the present.

"Your idea of a tour through the city is more like a fifty-yard dash, isn't it?" he quipped.

"I. . .we had to get away."

Her words came breathlessly, and Peter realized his hands still framed her slim waist. But then, hers also still rested at his.

"Ahem."

The clearly disapproving sound startled them, and they turned their heads to see who shared the building. Peter saw they stood inside a haberdashery. Colorful ribbons filled the shelves, and bolts of material stood along the papered walls. The gray-haired woman behind the counter raised her eyebrows.

"Were you in need of sewing items?" she asked, a frost to her voice as she eyed them.

Peter released his hold on Missy, and she did likewise, both of them self-conscious as they put space between them.

"Thank you, no." Missy touched the back of her hat, straightening it. "We're just, um, taking a breath to rest."

"A breath to rest?" the woman repeated.

Peter raised his brows at Missy's choice of words, but her attention had gone to the shop's sole window. She peered beyond the white letters painted on the glass as if searching for something. Peter looked too, but nothing struck him as out of the ordinary. After a moment she exhaled a long, relieved sigh and turned to Peter. "It's safe now."

"Safe?"

36

"I'll tell you. Later." Her eyes flicked to the woman then back to him in a silent message. "Say, are you thirsty? How about an ice-cream soda? Do they have those in England?" With a smile, she walked outside, not waiting for his reply. Peter had no choice but to follow, though curiosity ate at him to understand her unusual behavior.

"There's a drugstore not far from here. I know the soda jerk who runs the fountain. We can walk." She headed in the direction from which they'd come.

"All right." Peter fell into step beside her, deciding to practice patience.

The next shop they entered sported a long counter with three high stools near one wall. A balding man in an apron stood in the narrow area of working space between the counter and an array of machinery, one with spigots. On either side, tall glasses stood in neat stacks.

"Hello, Melissa. The usual for you today?"

"Yes, thanks, Jim. For my friend here, too." She looked at Peter. "You don't mind if I order for you?"

"Not at all." Peter took a seat on one of the high stools, hoping he would like the "usual" as well as he liked spaghetti. He watched the man fill a cup from one of the spigots, add ice cream and syrup, put a lid on it, then shake it. He poured the mixture into one of the glasses and set it in front of Missy. She picked up a spoon and dipped into it. "Mmm. Perfect as always, Jim."

The man nodded with a smile and set about making another. Peter looked around the shop. Pharmaceutical items lined the shelves. Illustrated signs advertising cough elixirs and tonics plastered the walls.

He studied the brown liquid in the glass set in front of him, hoping "the usual" didn't contain any medicines.

"It's not some dark, foul-tasting potion," Missy teased. "Go on. Try it."

Peter took a bite. The zippy flavor blended with the ice

cream to produce a pleasant taste. Well, if it was medicinal, at least it couldn't do him any harm.

"I take it you don't have soda fountains in England."

"I've never seen one. We live outside London, actually, and the surroundings are more rural." He thought of the verdant hills and dells, the slower pace of living, and the old-world flavor of the castles and manors. Quite unexpectedly, he found himself missing home.

"You have such a sad look on your face, all of a sudden."

"It's nothing, really." He smiled to reassure her. "Have you had your 'breath of rest'? Can you tell me what happened out there now?"

"Oh, yes. That." She fiddled with her glass, obviously flustered. Jim had moved to a back room, and they had the place to themselves. "Peter, I'm going to be completely honest with you, since you were so open with me when we met." She made a number of revolutions with her spoon through her soda then blew out a frustrated breath. Her blue eyes turned to his. "Where you come from, are there any gangsters?"

"Gangsters?" he asked, puzzled she should ask such a question.

"Men that are from the underworld, lawbreakers, mobsters, racketeers. . ."

"Yes, I know what they are. I imagine every society has men who choose a life of crime." He gave a slight shake of his head, not understanding where this was leading.

"I suppose. But Prohibition has only made things worse. The gangsters once committed their crimes behind the scenes; now they've come into the open, with drive-by shootings and such. They still try to hide a lot of it, like with the speakeasies, but very few of them are ever brought to justice."

Peter waited, hoping this would make sense soon.

"For years, a few members from one of those crime families have frequented my uncle Tony's restaurant. A man named Vittorio Piccoli is the mob boss, though as far as I know, he's never been to the restaurant. But his nephew Guido has, and he's taken an interest in me. He used to watch me when I was younger. I could always feel his eyes on me, and—" She pulled at her lower lip with her teeth. "Well, he's done watching. Let's just put it that way."

"Guido sent the candy," Peter inserted, beginning to understand.

She nodded. "I saw his car, and that's why I ran. I didn't want him to see me."

Something about her attitude gave him pause. "Do you have any ties to him, former or otherwise?"

"No. None at all. Only in his mind."

Her low, emphatic words erased the lingering doubt that she belonged to another, and he nodded.

"I thought you should know, since I'm palling around with you for a while. He, um, jealously guards whatever's his, and even though I'm not—his, I mean—things could get tricky."

"You're telling me I could be in danger."

"Yes." She gave a nervous shrug. "Not that I think you're the type to be intimidated, but I feel it's only fair to warn you. Vittorio's family isn't above murder to get what they want."

Though she'd acted with such independence, her eyes told all now. Fear touched the blue depths, making her vulnerable. A desire to protect her welled up inside him, and Peter covered her hand with his own. "Missy, I'm not without my own devices."

She looked doubtfully at his cane. "Wood wouldn't hold up well against bullets."

"Bullets?"

"Oh, yes. Tommy guns, revolvers—Vittorio and his bunch use them all."

He considered. "Perhaps it would be wise to invest in a handgun for protection." At her look of surprise, he explained, "I am well-versed in how to handle weaponry; from the time I was a boy, I was taught to shoot and hunt."

"My uncle Tony has a revolver; I could ask him."

He gave a nod of assent, then noticed her brow pucker with worry again.

"Don't be alarmed; when you're with me, I'll take care of you." He squeezed her hand in reassurance before letting go. "And I'm not frightened of Guido and his henchmen either."

"You really aren't, are you?" Puzzled wonder replaced the doubt in her eyes. "I'm not sure if that makes you the worst fool or the bravest man in New York City. But somehow, I believe what you say."

They shared a quiet smile tinged with hope. Jim returned to the counter, and Missy straightened on her stool.

"So let's have a look at that list again." She unfolded the paper, studied it, then smiled. "Peter, have you ever been to the movies?"

&

Their visit to the huge edifice that housed the motion-picture theater yielded no results. Hannah Metzler was absent that afternoon, but the woman at the ticket counter assured them she would be in to work the next day. When they couldn't locate the man who lived in Queens either, Peter decided to postpone the search. At Missy's invitation to stay and eat dinner at the restaurant, he politely declined. He didn't want to intrude on her generosity and time any more than he already had. Besides, he was exhausted. Lying down for an hour might help his mental acuity, which had begun to suffer.

Inside his luxurious hotel room, Peter removed his coat and shoes. He stared at his misshapen foot inside its wool sock and thought back to those grueling days after the disaster. Frostbite had destroyed part of his foot, and doctors had amputated two toes to save it. At the age of seven, he had learned to walk again, at first using a crutch, and later, as a young man, switching to a cane. Rather than grow embittered by his losses, he relied on humor to pull him through. His "angelic face," so called by his mother Annabelle, and his ready wit drew people to him even then. After mere minutes in his company, those who first pitied him forgot their sympathy and treated him as an equal. He'd been blessed with a great deal of love and support from his adoptive parents, which helped Peter not only to accept his situation, but also to deny self-pity and live each day to the fullest. Without Lawrence and Annabelle in his life, he might never have pulled through those trying days.

Peter stretched out upon the four-poster bed, his head cradled in the cloud of his feather pillow, and closed his eyes. Soon his thoughts faded away to nothing.

❧

Inside corridor after empty corridor, Peter moved along the carpet as ice-cold water swirled around his bare ankles.

"Mummy?" Gaslights above flashed all around him, flickered, and went out. Incandescent fog metamorphosed into obscure shadows. "Mummy?"

Suddenly he was back in his stateroom, shivering in his nightshirt, awakened from sleep by his mother's insistent hand on his shoulder.

"Come, Peter. You must wake up."

"Why, Mummy?" He rubbed the sleep from his eyes and yawned. She stood before him, beautiful as ever in her brown and gold evening gown. Her dark hair was piled in ringlets atop her head but mussed. Her blue eyes were fearful and teary, though she remained calm.

"We must leave the ship. We're taking another boat."

"I'm tired."

"Not now, my pigeon. Stop your whining. You can go back to sleep soon." She hurried around the stateroom as she spoke, collecting his discarded knickers, shirt, and shoes. All of a sudden, she stopped, as if frozen, and dropped them all to the carpet. Her shoulders began to shake.

"Mummy?"

Outside the cabin, he heard shouting, crying. A heavy knock cracked the door, and she swung her gaze toward it in fear.

"Mummy?"

"You must always remember, Peter." She knelt in front of him as he stood with his back to a corridor wall. She slipped the locket over his head. Her eyes drilled into his. "It is important that you never forget. It is your destiny! Do you understand, Peter? It is what brought us here. . . ."

Destiny brought us. . . .

Do you understand Peter?

It is what brought us here. . . .

Destiny brought us. . . .

Abruptly caught up in a whirlpool of icy water, he was sucked down, alone, deep into a swirling mass of black ocean. He opened his mouth in a silent scream, shards of cold stinging his skin.

Mummy!

❧

With a jerk, Peter awoke, sitting bolt upright on the hotel bed. His face had broken out in a sweat, and he struggled to regain even breaths. Eyes wide, he braced his hands on the mattress, trembling, remembering. The dream had always ended after the knock at the door, forcing him awake. This time, there had been more.

Missy's echo yesterday of his mother's words had jarred loose the memory of that night on the boat. He could still feel how his mother's eyes had bored into his as she placed the locket around his neck.

She had said it was his destiny. What was his destiny? What had Mother wanted him to remember?

His hand still shook as he checked his pocket watch. He had slept more than three hours. No outside glow muted his curtains; the sky had grown dark.

Food held no appeal; instead, he reflected on all Missy and Mr. Delaney had told him, the latter of which had been precious little. His gaze shifted to his valise, which held another item of worth. He turned on a light and retrieved the small box from where he'd secured it. He opened it, pouring a cascade of diamonds into his palm. The light stoked multi-sparkles in the facets. Only a fool would keep such a necklace in his room, and with all the talk of crime and gangsters, he didn't dare carry it on his person. Deciding to learn if the hotel had a safe, he replaced the jewelry in its simple cardboard box, dressed, and headed for the lobby.

Once he'd learned all he could in Manhattan, before he secured passage on a ship back to Liverpool, he would embark on the peculiar mission asked of him last week. Until that time, he planned to focus every waking moment on his own personal quest. Somehow, he must find the answers.

five

Melissa was ready when Peter came to collect her the next day. He seemed quieter than usual, more intense, somehow, and eager to get started. Once they'd hailed a cab and climbed inside, she studied him.

"Is everything all right?"

"Hm?" He glanced at her as if wondering what she meant. "Oh, yes. Everything's chipper."

"Why don't I believe you?"

He chuckled. "All right, then. I had the dream last night. The one about the *Titanic.*"

"Oh?" She hesitated to delve further, feeling like an interloper, though he'd offered the information.

"Yes. Strangely, your words from the first day in the restaurant mirrored the words in my dream. My mother told me destiny brought us here. I assume she meant to New York, that is, if the recollection of your words didn't spark an addition to my dream. I remembered her placing the locket around my neck, so I'm inclined to believe she did say those words."

Melissa furrowed her brow, sharing his frustration and pain. "As time progresses, you'll remember more, Peter. I'm sure of it. Just look at how much you've discovered in two days."

"I know. I must exercise patience. I've been ignorant of the truth for sixteen years. I can surely tolerate a few more days or weeks. Even months."

That he might extend his stay in Manhattan filled Melissa with pleasure. She remembered how he'd held her so close after their narrow escape the day before. She had thought Peter might even try to kiss her as they'd stood inside the entrance of the haberdashery, his large hands at her waist. She'd felt lost in his intense eyes and wasn't entirely sure she would have stopped him had he tried. Putting a rein on that memory, she then recalled the revelation that had stunned her before their mad dash down the sidewalk. Melissa opened her mouth to ask the question about Annabelle, but Peter spoke first.

"You never speak of your parents. Are they still living?"

"My mother is, but not my father." She worked to keep the chill out of her voice.

"Does your mother live in Manhattan?"

"No." The cab pulled up at the Roxy Theater and saved Melissa from having to explain. "Ah, here we are," she said brightly.

Distracted, Peter stared at the enormous edifice, of which they'd only viewed the lobby the day before.

"Wait 'til you see the inside," Melissa said.

She led him through the modest entrance and on into a cavernous lobby. An imitation galaxy of thousands of marquee lights glimmered from the foyer ceiling. Grecian statues lined the walls. In its gilt frame, an illustrated poster featured the Warner Brothers movie *Lights of New York*, and Melissa turned to him in excitement. "It's the first motion picture talkie all the way through."

"Talkie?"

"Not silent—it has sound and music."

"You've seen it?"

She shook her head. "It says so on the poster."

"Ah, yes." Peter noted the captions. "Well, once we've spoken to Mrs. Metzler, perhaps we should investigate as long as we're here. I've yet to see a motion picture."

Her heart jumped. This was beginning to seem much like a date, and she had mixed feelings about such a notion. But she gave an nod, and they headed into the theater. Upon querying a man in uniform, they learned Mrs. Metzler was cleaning in the auditorium. The movie wasn't set to show for another hour, but Peter secured tickets. After they gave their reasons for needing to enter the theater early, the manager gave them permission. Once they walked through the doors, their feet sank deeply into plush carpeting. Peter stopped and revolved in a slow circle to take in his surroundings.

"My word."

"I'm surprised you're impressed." Their voices echoed in the spacious arena, which housed thousands of seats on multi-tiered levels. "Surely the castles in England are much more awe-inspiring."

"The castles in England are homes to the nobility. This public movie house is a *cathedral*. And your department store was also quite lavish."

She giggled. "New York City, for all her crime, certainly knows how to put on the Ritz with sparkle and glamour, I'll give her that. I've heard it said when they built the Roxy last year, they dubbed it the Cathedral of the Motion Picture."

"Not a difficult stretch of the imagination to reason why."

Mammoth curtains fronted the wide stage, and gilded stairways flanked either side. Urns bedecked numerous alcoves along the scrolled walls of the dual balconies, and costly drapery adorned the space behind each one. Opulent acres of lush carpeting spread out before them. An enormous crystal chandelier that must weigh tons gleamed high within the domed ceiling and cast twinkles of shimmering light over the huge rotunda.

Melissa noticed two women polishing seats nearby. "Peter."

He turned from studying the stage, and she motioned toward the women.

Set on his course again, he walked toward the workers, and Melissa followed. Upon inquiry, they located a small, buxom woman who proved to be Hannah Metzler, polishing near the stage with another woman. Unfortunately they also found Mrs. Metzler spoke little English. Regardless, Peter pulled his mother's locket from his coat, but when he mentioned the *Titanic,* she grew agitated and spoke in a foreign language

Melissa didn't recognize. Tears swam to Mrs. Metzler's eyes. She rapidly patted her heart, shaking her head in denial, and hurried away from Peter and up the aisle.

"She lost all her family," the other woman explained with an accent not as pronounced. "She is one from third-class immigrants who survived, but her husband, her three sons. . ." The woman shook her head sadly.

Peter momentarily closed his eyes, his jaw working. "Please give her my most sincere apologies for troubling her."

"Yes, I do this. I hope you find what you seek," the woman said before turning back to her work.

He stared into space as if lost to his thoughts.

"Peter?" Melissa touched his sleeve. "Do you want to sit down?"

He nodded, giving her a shadow of a smile.

They chose a pair of seats midway to the stage. When he remained silent, Melissa laid her hand on his.

"Please, tell me what's troubling you."

❧

Peter took in a long breath and exhaled it softly. He propped his elbows on his legs. Steepling his fingers together, he lowered his forehead to them and rubbed his fingertips along his brow in a gesture of remorseful doubt.

"Peter?"

Missy's hand tentatively touched his back.

He straightened and looked at her. "I feel like the worst kind of heel for bringing to mind a tragedy that robbed so many of their lives. Yet conversely, I feel driven to pursue this. Am I wrong to do so?"

"It's only natural you'd want to find your family. Your reasons aren't selfish."

He shifted his gaze to the ornate wall of drapery hiding the stage. "At first, I'm ashamed to say, they were. I wanted to prove to a woman that I was worthy of her affections, though I myself wasn't certain if that were true. Being nameless in

English society isn't a desirable attribute when one wishes to marry." He chuckled wryly. "Yet since last night, since the dream, I find it's no longer all about Claire. My purpose has altered; I need to find these answers for me. To find where it is—who it is—I come from. Does that sound selfish?" He turned his head to look at her again.

She lowered her hand from his back. "No, it sounds human." She hesitated. "This woman, Claire. . .do you love her?"

Taken aback by the question, Peter tried to frame his answer. "Our families are acquaintances; we grew up together, attended the same balls and parties. My past, before the *Titanic*, was something about which we never spoke. We British are actually quite reserved and shield our secrets well." Which made it that much more amazing he was sharing his problems with her now. Yet he'd carried them alone for so long; it eased his soul to speak of them.

She gave a slight understanding nod. He sensed she had put distance between them, and regretted burdening her with his troubles. "Tell me of your family," he said suddenly, desiring to know.

Her eyes flickered with surprise. She averted her gaze to the seats in front of them, as if now wary. "What do you wish to know? You've already met my aunt Maria, and there's my uncle Tony. He was a widower when he met Aunt Maria. He's a kind man with an artist's soul. Both he and Maria have treated me like a daughter. My cousins—Tony's children from his first marriage—are younger than me. Lucio and Cecily. And Rosa is Maria and Tony's child. You'll meet them all soon, I'm sure."

"And your mother?" he asked softly.

"My mother?" she repeated bitterly, then gave a curt laugh. "I don't consider my mother part of my family."

His mouth opened in shock, and she looked down at her skirt.

"Maybe that sounds horrible, but she dumped me on Maria

when I was eight and ran off with the man who became her fourth husband. The don—Don Ortega, Maria's brother—was her third. I suppose I should be grateful; at least she didn't divorce my father. He died and escaped any likelihood of that happening."

Peter heard the pain underlying her tone. "Missy. I'm sorry."

"Don't be. Mama loved money and whoever had the means to give it to her more than she loved me. I've come to accept it. And I'm thankful for Maria; she was more of a mother to me than the woman who gave me life."

Unsure what to do to quell the tide of bitter hurt he'd unleashed with his unknowing words, Peter took hold of her hand. Startled, she looked at him.

"Forgive me for opening an old wound and for speaking when I have no right, but your absence in her life is most certainly her loss."

Her expression softened in wonder. "Why, Peter. That's so sweet. I. . .thank you." Her lips softly parted, and Peter lowered his gaze to them.

He wanted to kiss her.

Astonished by the sudden thought, he did nothing but lift his eyes to hers. What might have happened, he never found out. Voices startled them both to the present as more people entered the theater. Peter withdrew his hand from Missy's, then discovered he missed its warmth.

They talked of trivial matters until the curtain slid open and a hush filled the great rotunda. Silence fled as powerful notes of organ music resounded throughout the theater from a balcony high above. A film in black and white flickered across the screen. First, a cartoon entitled *Plane Crazy* featured an animated mouse named Mickey and was followed by a twenty-minute serial before the feature movie began. To Peter's consternation, he soon realized the talkie was a film about gangsters, and he looked over to Missy to see how she was taking it. Her expression was rigid, but when he whispered to her an offer to leave, she shook her head no.

The musical score included a blend of Tchaikovsky, Hebrew music, and popular ballads. Though the sound quality seemed unclear at times and tinny, he was nonetheless amazed to hear sound in a motion picture, to see a motion picture at all. Yet he couldn't enjoy it, not when Missy clearly was not. She jumped in her chair at the gunshots, and Peter could feel her tension crackling like electricity, which he suspected had nothing to do with the film. Finally, he took her hand and stood, leading her up the aisle and out of the theater.

"Peter?" she asked in bewilderment when they reached the lobby.

He stopped and turned toward her. "Tell me you wish to go back in there, and we will. But only if it's what you really want. And I suspect you don't."

She gave him a resigned half smile. "Am I that easy to read?"

Sensing her distress, he did his best to lighten the situation. "Not unless you make it a regular practice to embed nail prints into the chair cushions."

She chuckled. "Peter Caldwell, I like you."

"The feeling is mutual." He smiled. "Now would you like to go somewhere and get a bite to eat?"

"As long as it's not pasta." She laughed again, and he joined in. A doorman opened the door for them, and Peter waited for Missy to precede him onto the sidewalk.

"Well, well, if it isn't Melissa Reynolds."

At a woman's catty words, Peter turned to look behind them, as did Missy.

A brunette in a short, beaded, yellow dress that hung like a sack coolly returned Missy's gaze. Numerous strands of beads draped her neck. Along with the bright red lipstick she wore, the woman used paint on her face, a lot of it; unfortunately, it did nothing to smooth her features, made harsher by her cropped hair.

six

"Florence." Melissa managed a civil greeting, though her lips thinned when the flapper gave Peter a slow appraisal.

"Tall, not so dark, but oh-so-definitely handsome." Florence arched her brow. "Aren't you going to introduce me to your friend, Melissa?" Her attention never left his face.

Melissa would rather take him by the arm and haul him away, but courtesy demanded she honor the request. "Peter, this is Florence. Florence, Peter."

"Well, hel-looo, Peter." She took his hand to shake and, in Melissa's opinion, held it longer than necessary. "So, you new in town?"

"Just arrived from London, actually."

Florence squealed. "And just listen to that accent! A classy British gent, unless I miss my guess. But even gentlemen have their vices, eh?" She sidled closer. "If you're interested in the goods, I can score you some hooch."

"Hooch?"

"You know, booze. Liquor," she explained when he only shook his head in ignorance.

Melissa clenched her teeth at the bold flirtation Florence forced her to witness. "You're barking up the wrong tree, Florence. I suggest you go find a different one to yap at." She glanced at Peter. "We really should be leaving."

"Guido's not going to like it that you're out two-timing him," Florence sneered.

"I'm not two-timing anyone."

"No? He seems to think you two are an item, though why, I couldn't even begin to imagine." The sweep of Florence's cold gaze left no doubt in Melissa's mind that the flapper thought

Melissa not worth the trouble. If Melissa could convince Guido of that, she would gladly do so.

Instead of shooting off with another retort, Melissa took Peter by the arm as she'd wanted to do in the first place, turned her back on Florence, and resumed walking toward the streetcar stop.

"Did you just call me a tree?" Peter asked.

Despite her annoyance, Melissa smiled. "An American expression. I told her to leave you alone, more or less." Suddenly she realized how that could be taken. "Believe me. You don't want to get involved with bootleggers."

"I have no intention of doing so."

"I'm glad to hear it." She hadn't thought him the type to be interested in obtaining illegal liquor. "About what happened back there—I'm sorry about Florence." The woman was no friend, but Melissa felt an apology was in order regarding Florence's brazen behavior.

"Don't be concerned. It's nothing new to me, though her particular mode of fashion isn't something I'm accustomed to seeing in England."

An odd prick of resentment toward those unknown women needled Melissa. Nothing new? She gave him a sidelong glance. Well, why should she be surprised others found him attractive? And didn't he tell her he was almost engaged? Her mind wandered further. That woman rejected him, but he must feel strongly about her, must care deeply to have asked her to marry him. The idea discouraged her, and Melissa put a swift check on such thoughts. Maria had been right to warn her this morning. To curb this nonsense, she pointedly chose to introduce the subject of his girlfriend.

"Tell me about Claire."

He looked at her in some surprise. "Claire?" he asked as if he'd forgotten her name. "What do you wish to know?"

That seemed an odd response. Didn't people in love look for each and every opportunity to praise the attributes of the one to whom their heart was linked? Her cousins did; as for Melissa, she'd never been in love so didn't know.

"Is she pretty?"

"Yes, quite so. Beautiful actually."

"Mm. That's nice." His answer didn't improve Melissa's frame of mind. "I assume her family is also titled?"

"Her father holds a seat in the House of Lords, as does my own."

"Ah." She didn't know much about British aristocracy, except that the king ruled England, but Peter's reference to the House of Lords sounded very regal.

She tried to think up another question to ask about Claire, then realized she didn't really want to know.

"So, if your father is in the House of Lords now, that means you'll be taking his place one day. Right?"

"No, that honor will go to my younger brother."

"Your younger brother?" She may not understand much about the peerage, but she did know the eldest was supposed to inherit. At least that's how it happened in most societies she'd read about. She assumed Peter was the eldest since his parents had both adopted him and married after the *Titanic* disaster.

They came to a stop where the streetcar would collect them. He looked at her then. "I'm not a blood heir, so I cannot inherit the title or any of the privileges that come with it." Not an ounce of regret filled his words. "Edward will make a fine earl when that day arrives; he's viscount now."

"And what about you, Peter? What will you do?"

"Do?"

"Once your mission is done here? Once you leave New York."

"Why, I'll go back to England, of course."

"Of course."

Thankfully the streetcar rattled up to them on its tracks, and Melissa turned her face away to hide the flames she knew burned her cheeks. But she couldn't put a brake on the sudden hope that hurtled through her mind of wishing that day would never come.

❧

Not desiring to be rude and reject a second dinner invitation, Peter acquiesced to Missy's request that he dine at the restaurant. Once he escorted her home, he returned to his hotel room to change into evening wear and afterward took time to jot a message to send home, assuring everyone he'd arrived safely and all was progressing well under the circumstances.

His mother had worried when she learned he would embark on a voyage to America. If the memory of the *Titanic* disaster had been as vivid to him as it was to her, he might have felt the same and avoided ocean travel. Even without the full memory of that night, it had taken a good deal of fortitude to board a vessel that traveled the same route as the *Titanic*.

As the first ribbons of sunset unfurled over the bustling city, Peter entered Marelli's. Amazed to see the restaurant teeming with life, he stood in the entrance to absorb the difference.

Patrons filled almost every table, and poignant music rippled from the strings of the violin played by a dark, mustachioed man with superlative talent. A single globed candle glowed on each table of the darkened room. Delicious spicy aromas brought the air to life, reminding Peter he'd not eaten since lunch.

A young girl, possibly fourteen, with long curly dark hair and wearing a frilly white blouse and long black skirt came up to him.

"Allo, you must be Melissa's Peter." She giggled. "I am Rosa, Maria and Tony's daughter. Come, we have a special table reserved for you."

A special table? Peter followed the girl to a booth near the back of the restaurant where the musician played. Fronds of plants atop the ledges brought a feeling of the outdoors to the surrounding booths. Each private cubicle gave the mood of a clandestine meeting.

Once seated, he glanced around the restaurant, failing to see a familiar face. "Is Missy in the vicinity?"

Rosa handed him a menu with a shy smile. "She asked that I take care of you. She will be out soon."

"Thank you."

"My pleasure." She giggled again, moving away.

Peter smiled and opened the menu to peruse the Italian cuisine. He debated trying something different this time. Perhaps the fettuccine Alfredo or the *caponata,* described as a spicy eggplant dish, or even the *baccalà* dish of salted cod. As he weighed the choices, Rosa returned bearing a platter with huge hunks of what Peter had learned was mozzarella cheese. In her other hand, she carried a plate with a crusty loaf of fresh-baked bread and set both before him.

He ordered the fettuccine Alfredo, deciding to live adventurously and sample a new entrée each time he came. He hadn't intended to make a habit of dining here since the Waldorf-Astoria also boasted fine culinary establishments, but here the food rated superb, the atmosphere was always pleasant, and the Marellis were a friendly lot. Not to mention that Missy was a person he would like to know better.

The violinist ended his performance, taking a seat at a nearby table. A boy appeared with a guitar and perched on the edge of a stool. Then Peter saw Missy and forgot all about food.

Looking as if she'd been immersed in a moonbeam, Missy moved to stand beside the guitar player, who settled the instrument across his knee. Her white lace blouse shimmered, matching the string of pearls at her throat and in her ears. A dark skirt flowed over her slim waist and hips, offsetting her fair beauty. Her face glowed like dew under the moonlight; her hair glimmered like radiant stars. Peter reasoned the white spotlight added to the ethereal effect, but he was nevertheless amazed.

The guitar player strummed the strings softly, producing the most beautiful, haunting music that heated Peter's blood and brought chills to his skin. Missy began to sing, and the chills increased. Peter stared, totally bedazzled, his mouth falling open.

A hint of sultriness laced the sweetness of her voice, the drawn-out notes clear and strong, at the same time muted and soft. Peter didn't understand the foreign words, Italian or Spanish, but he judged from the wistful expression on her face that this must be a song about love. She put all of herself into her aria, which seemed to nestle into his heart and make its home there.

Once the last soft note wavered into oblivion, Peter could only continue to stare. Enthusiastic applause burst forth all around him, and he realized it wasn't her uncle Tony's prowess with the violin that brought patrons to this restaurant as Missy had said, or even the guitar player, as skillful as he'd been; Missy was the sparkling lure that captured their clientele.

She smiled her thanks to the audience, then noticed Peter and moved his way, but he couldn't seem to wrap his mind around the present. Couldn't remember when he'd heard such an exquisite voice. The greeting that fell off his tongue seemed lackluster in comparison to the uplifting experience that still buoyed his heart.

"That was lovely."

"Thank you." She inclined her head shyly. "May I sit down?"

Her words reminded Peter of his uncommon bad manners. "Of course, please do." He stood as he spoke, jarring the table and causing the flame in the candle to shiver.

She gave a delicate laugh. "Please, Peter. Sit down and enjoy your meal."

"Will you join me? For dinner, I mean."

She hesitated the barest moment. "I'd love to."

"I've already ordered, so once you decide, you'll have to tell Rosa." He almost groaned at his ineptitude; she did after all know the workings of their family restaurant far better than he did.

"Rosa knows what to bring me." Her words were gracious; her manner kind. "Before I forget, I want to ask if you'd like to attend services with us tomorrow."

"Services?"

"Church. Tomorrow *is* Sunday."

"Of course. And yes, thank you. I would." He was beginning to resemble a callow youth out for his first night in high society. Deciding it would be in his best interest to put the bread and cheese to good use and engage his mouth, Peter took a portion of both.

"The song, it was beautiful," he said when he'd gathered his wits about him enough to speak again.

"It's a Latin song of love; the boy who played guitar is Lucio, my uncle Tony's son. He's very skilled."

"Yes, he is. Have you had training? You sound as if you have."

The violin player strode to the table, preempting her answer. A stocky man of medium height, he bore the dark coloring and lively dark eyes of all the Italians Peter had met. "You must be Peter," he said, his accent strong. He thrust out his hand in greeting. "Welcome to our humble restaurant," he said as he shook Peter's hand.

"You have a wonderful place."

"*Grazi, grazi.* Please, sit down. My Maria has told me some of your story. I hope all turns out well for you."

He spoke with them a few minutes more before his attention shifted to another table, and he moved that way to speak with the two men there.

"Your family is quite grand."

"Thank you. They've made me feel wanted."

Her wistful eyes twisted his heart, and he felt he should change the subject. "Regarding my previous question—have you had vocal training?"

"No." Her eyes grew shuttered, and she tore away a hunk

of bread. "Mother sang in the Metropolitan Opera; I suppose that's the one trait she gave me, the ability to sing. . . . So tell me, does a visit to Coney Island sound good for Monday?" She bit into the bread.

"Yes, that sounds lovely." Her quick change of subject and forced smile told him the subject of her mother wasn't open to discussion. He couldn't help but see the irony: He endeavored to do all within his power to gather information about his mother, while Missy worked with equal fervor to dispense with the memory of hers. Perhaps this quest would help them both lay their ghosts to rest.

seven

On Monday, Peter and Melissa paid a nickel apiece to take the subway to the famed New Yorkers' playground of Coney Island. After services the day before, she had suggested they make a day of it at Coney Island once they located Horace Miller, the man who could hold a key to Peter's locked past.

Peter enthusiastically agreed, yet when Melissa mentioned that many also found pleasure at the beach there and suggested they take advantage of the bathhouses to change clothes and indulge in a swim, he adamantly refused. After a gap of tense silence, he shared with her the cause of his crippled state, stumbling over his sentences and avoiding her eyes as if sure she would be disgusted. But Melissa's feelings had been far from disgust, and when Peter looked up, his eyes opened wider to see the tears that trickled down her cheeks.

"Missy?"

"You went through so much," she had explained, "for one so young. More than many of us had to bear."

To her shock, he had lifted his hand and wiped away her tear with the pad of his thumb. "Don't cry for me." His smile had been encouraging. "Long ago I accepted the things I couldn't change. I'm all right. Really."

She had nodded, his touch and tender expression doing strange things to her heart and robbing her of her voice.

Now, she watched him as they exited the subway and he studied their surroundings with curious interest. Her sundry difficulties couldn't begin to compare with the great travail he'd suffered, yet he so often seemed without a care, as he did now. She wished she could exhibit optimism despite all odds. Even as they approached the Bowery, the four-block alley running from Steeplechase to Feltman's Arcade, delight animated Peter's face at the overabundance of glitzy penny arcades and open game booths that challenged a man's skill while encouraging him to empty his pockets of nickels. Bordering this were terrifying rides that brought shivers of fear and screams of delight from their passengers.

Mechanical pianos played swinging jazz numbers and vied with the shouts of barkers calling over each other to attract prospective customers. Concession stands offered an assortment of tempting foods, and the mouthwatering aroma of fire-roasted hot dogs and warm bread wafted through the air.

"First, we should find Mr. Miller," Peter said.

He spoke as if he would say more. When he didn't continue, Melissa prodded, "And then?"

"And then. . ." He gave her a sidelong glance, his boyish smile in place. "We play."

Melissa giggled, not surprised that she'd been correct in her assessment of his character and that he was still a boy at heart.

After asking directions from a hot-dog vendor, they found the shooting gallery where Horace Miller spun his spiel, encouraging passersby to engage in hitting his targets. Painted metal ducks ran past on a mechanical track at the far end of the booth. Mr. Miller, a brown derby rakishly angled over his high brow, eyed Peter and Melissa like a snake would field mice.

"Well, sir," he said, appraising Peter, "you look like a gent who can handle a rifle well. Step right up and try your luck. Only ten cents for ten shots; hit half the targets, and you can win your lady a gen-u-ine Kewpie doll."

"Actually, I was hoping you could help me in another area. I'm here to seek out information. Am I correct in presuming that you're Mr. Miller?"

The man's gregarious attitude hardened to coldness. "You're not here to take a shot?"

"No."

"Then beat it." He swung his thumb to the side for them to go.

"I just want to ask a couple of questions; I won't take much of your time, only a few minutes."

"What are you, some kind of cop? I ain't got the time to say nothin' to no copper."

"I'm not a cop. I understand you sailed on the *Titanic*, and I seek information, to discover anything you can tell me about this woman." Peter withdrew the locket.

At Peter's mention of the ship, the man's eyes livened with a flash of shock, then narrowed. "Look, bub, you want me to look at that there picture, then you lay out a dime."

Peter nodded and extracted the coin, setting it on the waist-high wooden planking between them.

The man pocketed the coin and held out his hand for the locket. Peter hesitated before handing it to him. Mr. Miller took a long look at it. "Can't say as I recall anyone like her in third class, but then it's been awhile."

"You were in third class?" Peter asked.

"Yeah." The man grew embittered as he returned the locket. "I was one of them gutter rats who made it. They wouldn't let us immigrants up 'til all the swells had been taken care of. Even our women and children were left below, locked in like animals. By the time they allowed us up, most of the lifeboats were gone. More of our women and children were lost than saved."

Melissa sensed by the man's attitude that his words were personal. "Did you lose someone close, Mr. Miller?"

Her quiet words, the first words she'd spoken, made him swing his attention her way. He stared a moment, and his face slackened. "My grandmother. She was so sure that coming to America would be the start of a great new life. It's all she talked about for years."

"I'm so sorry for your loss."

Her sincere words produced a faint nod, the hint of a smile, before he turned to Peter and handed him a rifle. "You gonna take that shot or not?"

"It's not necessary. Thank you for your time." As Peter turned away, Melissa caught his eye and gave a slight tilt of her head toward the booth, sensing that his cooperation might give the barker a boost. Peter looked at her a moment, then turned back. "On second thought, I will take a shot."

Melissa watched as he leaned his cane against the booth, lifted the rifle, and took careful aim. Five rapid explosions knocked five ducks down with loud metal pings. A few passersby stopped to stare in amazement.

Both the barker and Melissa turned to Peter, their mouths agape.

He handed back the rifle and shrugged, his expression self-conscious as he faced Melissa. "I did mention that I learned to hunt."

※

While others vied for a place in line to try their chance at shooting the metal ducks, Peter took Missy's arm and steered her through the crowd. They walked close, but Peter sensed her distance and wondered what was running through her mind. The shooting gallery had required a simple aim really, nowhere near as difficult as the clay pigeons catapulted into the air which he'd mastered as a lad. Yet Peter now felt perhaps he should have purposely missed a couple of the targets, though Missy had accepted the Kewpie doll with a grateful smile.

He worked to cover his own disappointment. He'd known all along that on a ship of more than two thousand souls, bearing three different classes, the likelihood of finding even one of six people on the list who might have known his mother was slim to nothing. Still, he had hoped for some information by this time.

From her excited words of the previous day, Peter knew Missy wanted to partake in the fun of Coney Island. Peter could also use the relaxation. He made a choice to take pleasure in this day spread out before them and in this fantasy land thickly riddled with roller coasters, Ferris wheels, carousels, and other alluring rides that promised to make one's heart soar one instant, then drop the next.

He smiled at Missy. "What do you wish to do first?"

"First?" The gaiety of their surroundings began to take hold, and her eyes sparkled. "I noticed a house of mirrors earlier; I'd like to go there."

"Then go there, we shall." He formally crooked out his arm toward her, and smiling, she wrapped hers through it.

As lighthearted as children, they wended their way through aisles of warped mirrors that stood taller than they did and laughed at their crazy reflections. Afterward, they lived dangerously and rode the Cyclone, a roller coaster whose tracks spiraled into a figure eight with plummets at terrific speed. Once they exited the train of linked cars, it took them both awhile to find their balance again, then they decided to eat lunch.

For a penny a piece, they feasted on clams drenched in butter at one of the many restaurants. They spoke of nothing and everything and, as if in silent accord, made no mention of the *Titanic* or of their quest or of gangsters. This remained a day to be enjoyed, and they both shed their troubles and took in all they could of the innumerable amusements.

If Peter had secured a room in one of the plush hotels nearby and stayed a week, he still wouldn't have covered all that Coney Island had to offer. They visited a house of wax and braved various rides, staying away from the seedier establishments, the havens to gamblers and those of low morals.

The setting sun highlighted the clouds with bright pink as they, along with hundreds of others, promenaded along the wide boardwalk that stretched over half the length of the area. To the right, a strip of brown beach ran alongside, and a number of bathers took advantage of the Atlantic Ocean.

When they grew weary of walking, they stopped at Feltman's Pavilion for Mr. Feltman's famed invention of pork sausages encased in rolls. The hot dogs took the edge off their hunger, and afterward, they rode a carousel of painted horses. By the time they left the pavilion, the sky had darkened to faded ink, but Coney Island was lit up as if it were Christmas. Hundreds of thousands of bright electrical lights rimmed the massive rides and fanciful towers, spires, and minarets on the Oriental-style buildings.

They walked along with the crowds, carried away by the magic of Coney Island as they observed the blur of activity around them.

"Are you willing to try one more ride before we take the subway home?" Missy asked, a twinkle in her eye.

"Of course."

Eagerly, she took Peter's hand and led him through the crowd to the towering Wonder Wheel. It stood like a revolving beacon beside the ocean, the ride brightly lit up with hundreds of incandescent lights. Deciding against one of the inside cars that slid on curved tracks toward the center and then back with each revolution of the wheel, they opted instead for one of eight stationary cars that rimmed the outside of the monstrous Ferris wheel. Evidently, their choice of seating wasn't popular, for when the attendant couldn't find two more takers to the stationary car, he closed their door.

The wheel hoisted them higher into the air, then stopped as people boarded the lower cars. Finally, they reached the top, the wheel coming to a swift halt again.

Missy exhaled a breath. "Oh, Peter, look."

All of Coney Island lay spread out before them, a glittering panorama of festive white lights against a backdrop of dark ocean and sky. "It's like a fairy tale," she exulted softly.

They sat close on one side of the car. She turned to look at him at the same moment he looked at her, their faces only inches apart.

Wrapped inside the magic of their surroundings, they stared at one another. His gaze flicked down to her lips, then slowly returned to the oasis of her blue eyes. Her lips softly parted, and he lifted his fingertips to skim her silken jaw. "A fairy tale," he repeated on a whisper, lowering his head toward hers as he moved his hand away.

Before their lips could touch, the wheel gave a sudden lurch and went into motion. Peter drew back, stunned by both actions. Uneasy and a trifle embarrassed, he shifted position, averting his attention to the nighttime playground. A span of electric silence charged the air between them, while outside their car, people shrieked from the inside cars zipping along their tracks. Organ music played somewhere far below, but up so near the stars, all seemed muted.

Missy cleared her throat. "I. . ." Her words trailed off, as if she'd lost them.

Uncomfortable to discuss what had almost happened between them, Peter took the advantage. "After this ride has ended, we should return to Manhattan. It's late, and I want to get an early start in the morning."

"About that. . ." She looked down at her skirt and cupped one knee, digging her fingers into it nervously. "I can't go with you tomorrow."

"I see."

"It's not that I don't want to." Swiftly she met his gaze. "I promised my aunt I would help her with some things around the restaurant."

"I understand. You don't have to explain, Missy."

Peter changed the subject and soon had her laughing again, though he sensed her mood was forced. When he dropped her off at the restaurant, he knew something had altered between them but didn't dwell on the situation until he reached the solitude of his hotel room.

He regretted both his spontaneous attempt to kiss her and his lack of success in that attempt. But this time, any pang of guilt that prodded his conscience, whispering that he'd betrayed Claire, seemed far more subdued than before. As Peter lay stretched out on the bed, studying the carved ceiling, he began to question his situation. For weeks he'd dwelt on the past and what resolution it might unleash, but now he pondered his future and what mysteries it might contain. And to his shock, Claire was no longer a part of his personal aspirations.

eight

"Missy, if you scrub that spot any harder, you will dig through the floor and into the earth."

Melissa straightened from her crouched position on hands and knees and glanced at her aunt, who had just walked into the kitchen where Melissa scrubbed the floor. She dipped the scrub brush into the sudsy water again and continued scrubbing.

"Mi niña." Maria squatted beside her. "What is the matter?"

"Matter? Nothing's the matter. I thought you wanted the restaurant to have a thorough cleaning."

"Sí. But why today? You said you wanted to help Peter."

"I did." Melissa hesitated. "I do. I just felt it was time to get this done now. That's all."

Aunt Maria didn't force the issue but gave Melissa a concerned glance before she left the room. Melissa crawled to the next dry spot of flooring to give it a scrupulous cleaning with the bristles.

She didn't know what bothered her. Well, yes she did. When Peter had almost kissed her on the Ferris wheel, the desire for his kiss astonished her, confused her, even alarmed her. She needed this time away from him to sort through her feelings. Things between them were going too fast for strangers who'd known each other only a matter of days, yet she felt as if she'd known him a lifetime. She had always shied away from the prospect of falling in love. Not that Melissa thought herself unlovable; through tender care over all these years, Maria had proven that Melissa was, indeed, worthy of love. Nor did Melissa worry she would fail at marriage, because she would never treat a man the selfish way her mother had treated her husbands.

No. Most of her unease stemmed from Guido and his

unwanted notice of her; he had singled her out to wait on him since she'd turned fourteen. As the years progressed, so had his attention toward her, and she feared what he might do to her and those she loved. But Peter was nothing like Guido. He was a gentleman—kind, funny, attractive. Yet didn't his heart belong to Claire? Wasn't his love for her what had brought him to America? Despite the fact that Claire had refused him, wasn't his main initiative for his quest to win her back?

Her heart conflicted, Melissa tried to link answers to questions that weren't hers to ask. She clenched her teeth and scrubbed the floor harder. If all that mattered to the woman was his name, Claire didn't deserve a man like Peter. But that didn't change the fact that soon, very soon, Peter would return to England, to his home and family, and to Claire, while Melissa would remain in New York, and life would resume its usual course.

The thought was not at all satisfying.

Melissa threw herself into her work all day. When evening came, she fell into bed exhausted, but morning brought no relief from her discontent. Noon came and went, and she looked up often, expecting Peter to enter the restaurant. He usually came well before noon, but it had rained earlier, and that had slowed traffic. As the day stretched on, Melissa realized he wasn't coming. Now instead of the distance she'd sought between them, she desired his presence.

She waited on tables that night, her attention going to the door every time it opened. Her work suffered, reflecting her turmoil. When she mistook an order and brought the wrong entrée to a table, the customer grew belligerent. Lucio signaled the time had come for her to sing, but her voice carried little of the life it normally possessed.

Alone in her bed, she brought the covers up to her chin and closed her eyes. "I've hurt him. I know I have. My stupid insecurities pushed him away. Please. . .let him come back." She wasn't aware she'd phrased her longing into a prayer until after she'd uttered it, and that made her think. She would like to believe what Maria taught, that God was a guiding force in people's lives, but too many disappointments clouded such hopes. A whisper from the past she wished to forget taunted the fringes of her mind.

"I haven't the time to be saddled down with a daughter; besides, Clark doesn't like children. You take her, Maria. She likes you."

Melissa closed her eyes, and a tear escaped.

The next day seemed endless. More rain fell, and again, Peter didn't come.

On the fourth day, Melissa attacked her duties with dogged resignation. He wasn't coming; she might as well accept it and resume her life. She readied tables with stark efficiency, took orders from the few customers who visited, and taste-tested sauces. She made no more mistakes, but neither did she smile, and Maria softly scolded her, reminding her that no customer liked a grouchy waitress. Her warning seemed odd, since the restaurant had served only two tables of guests, both parties now gone.

That afternoon, Melissa spread a clean cloth over a table, fixing it so it hung evenly. She bent at the waist to smooth out the wrinkles.

"Hello, Missy."

At the sound of Peter's voice, she jumped up and whirled around so fast she was surprised she didn't injure herself. The joyful relief upon seeing him almost had her rushing forward to hug him.

"Peter." She blinked. "I wasn't expecting you." Of all the things she wanted to say, that wasn't one of them.

"I'm sorry I haven't been around lately."

His voice sounded hoarse. She studied him further and noticed the dull haze in his eyes. "Are you all right?"

"I was ill, but I'm doing better now, thank you. The morning after we visited Coney Island, I caught a nasty bug. Today I didn't feel as if the entire world was in constant upheaval, so

I felt it safe to leave my room."

He'd been ill! She hadn't chased him away.

Relief gave way to concern as she moved forward. Without thinking twice, she pressed her fingers to his brow and frowned. "You still feel a bit feverish. You shouldn't have left your bed so soon."

As she retreated a step, he gave a slight lurch forward and grabbed the back of a chair. She grasped his arm to help support him.

"You can barely stand!"

"No, I'm all right, really." His actions jerky, he moved to sit down.

"No, you're not, Peter." Determined, she set her jaw. "You don't eat right, you barely sleep, and now you come out of your sickbed and into this damp cold." She softened her demeanor. "Peter, these people aren't going anywhere. I sincerely doubt they'll be moving away within the next week. Please, go back to your hotel room and get some rest. Ask them to bring you a bowl of chicken soup; it's a good remedy. If we had some here, I'd make it for you, but we don't have any chicken, only veal. We can resume the hunt when you're feeling better."

He opened his mouth to argue, but something in her expression must have stopped him for he gave a resigned nod. "All right. You win, Missy. I do feel better than I did, but I certainly could use more rest."

Glad that she'd persuaded him to see reason, she was nevertheless concerned that he'd given in so quickly. "Are you certain you can make it back to your hotel on your own?"

"I got here, didn't I?"

She breathed out a worried laugh. "Barely, from the looks of you." A sudden thought hit. "Lucio has to run some errands for my uncle. I'll ask him to accompany you to the hotel."

"I wouldn't wish to impose. I'll be all right."

"I insist. I wouldn't get a wink of sleep tonight otherwise."

She turned away to mask the sudden torrent of emotion at

the thought of him lying helpless in the street with the rain pounding down on him. "I'll go ask Lucio now. Stay put." She gave him a warning glance. "I mean it. I don't want to come back here and find you gone. Capisci?"

He nodded as if dazed, and Melissa wondered if her gentle order sounded as fraught with hidden meaning to him as it did to her. She didn't want him to go, not now or in the future. How long he remained in her life depended on the success of his quest, and Melissa felt a harsh twinge of guilt for her sudden wish that his search would never end.

❧

Peter recovered after two more days of bed rest. When he lay awake, he relived the memory of Missy's resolute plea that he take care of himself. In her eyes, he had seen reflected the same desire that brought him to the restaurant that afternoon. Perhaps he'd been foolish to attempt such an undertaking before he'd made a full recovery, and in retrospect, he hoped his thoughtless action hadn't contaminated anyone else.

But the quest that urged him on had equaled his longing to see her again, and his muddled mind hadn't been able to reason out the consequences. He had missed her company and had gone to her. What astounded him more was that she had missed him. He'd seen that truth written in her jubilant expression during those first few seconds when she'd swung around to face him. Heard its revelation in her quiet, emphatic words that he mustn't go.

He couldn't remember ever having missed Claire and, in fact, hadn't thought about her in days. A modicum of remorse gave way to a magnitude of doubt as he dwelt on the matter now.

A glance at his pocket watch showed him the day was fast getting away from him. Eager to embark on his quest and to see Missy again, he hailed a taxicab to take him to the restaurant.

Again, Missy's eyes sparkled upon seeing him. "You look wonderful," she breathed. "I mean, you seem so much more rested. Your color is good, too."

Her own color had heightened, and he smiled. "Are you agreeable to traveling to Long Island today to find Patience Arbunckle?"

"Oh, yes. You've already eaten?"

He nodded, and her grin grew wide. "Good. Let me get my coat."

They took a cab to Pennsylvania Station and from there boarded a train into Long Island. Looking out the window, Peter eyed the vista of beaches and boxlike suburban homes. A quiet haven nestled away, Long Island appeared nothing like Manhattan. No skyscrapers towered in almost every available space of sky as they did in the city. Mile after mile of uninterrupted countryside and beaches flew past the train window.

"You might already know this," Missy said from beside him, "but last year, Charles Lindbergh flew his *Spirit of St. Louis* nonstop from this island to Paris in the first transatlantic flight. All of Manhattan gave him a ticker-tape parade upon his return. My cousins and I went to see; it was quite something."

"I read about that and found it quite extraordinary. Perhaps one day passengers will fly across the ocean in airplanes instead of taking voyages on ships."

"Now, that would be interesting," Missy agreed. "But I find it unlikely that such an idea would catch on with the masses."

"Oh, I don't know." He grinned. "I would try it."

She regarded him with an assessing smile. "I believe you would."

They found directions to the small lakeside hotel where Patience Arbunckle resided, as easily as they found the woman who ran the place. Bearing a gregarious charm yet stately elegance, Patience and her friend, Beth Ryan, led them to a table overlooking Lake Ronkonkoma, and they sat down to take tea.

"Legend has it that the lake contains special healing powers," Patience stated as they looked out over its blue waters. "It was formed by a retreating glacier. Whether the claims are true or not, it brings tourists in by the droves, and naturally, I'm pleased with that. My grandfather built this hotel and once told me the lake is bottomless, but I confess, I've never tested the waters so wouldn't know. I'm not much of a swimmer." Her eyes twinkled. "Now, how can I help you, Mr. Caldwell? You mentioned on the telephone that your visit here today concerns the RMS *Titanic*."

"The *Titanic?*" Patience's friend Beth uttered in shock.

"Yes, I understand you were a passenger, Mrs. Arbunckle."

"A very young one," she explained. "I was fourteen then and traveling with my family. We had gone to Europe on vacation and were returning home."

Peter hesitated to ask the question uppermost in his mind. She must have sensed it, for she nodded sadly. "My mother, my sisters, and I, all of us were rescued. My father was one of the brave men who stayed behind. He had no choice; they wouldn't allow men inside the lifeboats. Not on our side of the ship; perhaps if we had been on the other side. . ." Her smile grew melancholy. "But then, there's no use speaking of the past and what can't be changed, is there?"

"Actually, I've come to ask you to remember, if it isn't too painful for you."

"Oh?" She regarded him with surprise. "Are you a writer?"

"No." He handed her the locket and motioned for her to open it. "That was my mother. I was hoping you might remember her face or having had any acquaintance with her."

"Oh, my. It's been so many years. I can barely remember what I ate for dinner last night." She gave a light laugh but studied the picture. She shook her head. "I'm sorry. Her face isn't familiar to me."

"I understand." Peter took the locket, no longer disappointed by the outcome, having half expected it. Sixteen years was too great a time for a person to remember a casual acquaintance aboard a ship of thousands.

"May I see it?" Miss Ryan held out her hand. Peter detected the lilt of an Irish accent in her words, but it was her tense manner that caught his attention.

Curious, he opened the locket and handed it to her across the table. She looked down and inhaled a startled gasp.

Alert to her obvious recognition, he asked, "Were you on the *Titanic?* Did you know her?"

"No. I'm sorry." Her sympathetic brown eyes grew troubled. "But a year ago, I worked for a family on the island, not far from this hotel. I'd run on hard times, and I took a job as one of their maids. Such a sad home it was. One of the most lavish on the island, but not a moment's peace or happiness could be found there. The poor woman drifted in her husband's shadow. He was quite the tyrant, you see, a steel magnate, and he could scare a person clear into next week."

Peter remained patient, though he wanted to hurry the woman along in her memory.

"My job was to clean the upstairs rooms, and one room was always kept locked, though I was given a skeleton key and required to clean it every day. I even had to change the bedding to keep it fresh! Well, I did what was expected of me, though I don't mind tellin' you every ghost story I'd ever heard went flyin' through my head when I was in that room. Some of the other maids said they'd heard quiet sobbing from behind the locked door, though I never did. But in that house, who can tell what goes on?"

She shivered. "Later I learned the room belonged to their only son. He was involved in an automobile accident the night before the *Carpathia* pulled into the harbor. The roads were slick with rain, and he lost control. He died two days later."

A sense of startled unreality grabbed hold of Peter as her gaze locked with his. "Naturally, since the locked room was never occupied, the whole situation piqued my curiosity. I can still vividly recall the items I dusted every day. You might say I committed them to memory. There was a photograph on the dresser that I remember in detail. This woman was in it, and she wore this very locket."

nine

"Peter, are you all right?"

Melissa hesitated, uncertain what to do to help him. Five minutes after leaving Mrs. Arbunckle's hotel, Peter still stood silent beside the lake, studying its waters as if trying to see far beneath them.

"Peter?" She moved his way, when he suddenly turned, startling her into stopping.

"All right? No, I'm not all right."

His feelings didn't surprise her, but that he aired them did. All former reserve disappeared as he bared his heart and soul to her. A haze of pain clouded his eyes.

"I put all my misgivings behind me and sailed across an entire ocean, only to discover that my father is dead."

"Were you hoping to find him alive?"

"Yes. Yes, I was. That might sound absurd under the circumstances; after all, he refused to have anything to do with my mother and myself. Otherwise, he wouldn't have been absent for all those years and would have had some place in our lives. Yet a part of me hoped that we might lay all misconceptions and hard feelings to rest. . .that we could surmount the difficulties."

Melissa's heart ached at the raw pain in his voice. "Peter, you don't know for sure that the family Miss Ryan worked for is your own."

Her attempt at encouragement fell flat as he sadly shook his head. "She recognized my mother from that picture."

"But it's been over a year since she worked at the Underhills. Perhaps the woman in the photograph only looked like your mother."

"She recognized the locket, too."

Melissa drew her brows together, thinking. "All right, then what about what she said—that their son was in an accident the night before the *Carpathia* pulled into port?"

"What about it?"

"Maybe he was going to meet the ship. To meet you."

"We don't know that for certain." Wary hope filled his voice.

"No, but the very fact Miss Ryan brought it up seems important. She'd obviously heard it mentioned when she worked there. The date coinciding with the *Carpathia*'s arrival must have significance for it even to be mentioned and linked to his accident."

He looked at her a long moment, then dipped his head and nodded in weary resignation. "It's possible. I'll give you that."

"You'll never know unless you ask them."

He gave a wry laugh. "Truer words were never spoken, yet what if my father was right and a scorpion lies beneath the rock I uncover? Perhaps the tiger will have its way after all, and the lady behind the door was only a boy's dream."

Melissa didn't understand his odd words and assumed he spoke of his adoptive father. How she wished these lake waters could heal the heart as well as the body! Both she and Peter could use a plunge. She moved toward him, putting her hand to his arm in silent support, and he turned to look at her.

"Whatever happens, you're not alone, Peter. Remember that."

His gaze took in every inch of her face, and she held her breath.

"I will."

☙

Twenty minutes later, as they stood at the front door of the sprawling mansion that belonged to the Underhills, Peter replayed Missy's encouraging words. A housekeeper answered the bell and at first refused to admit them, but Peter pleaded for an audience. His manner and clothes must have convinced her he was no peddler, for she told them to wait a moment and closed the door. Soon it opened again, wider this time, and she motioned for them to enter.

Peter worked to control his breathing, though his pulse rate threatened to skyrocket through the carved ceiling. This might all be merely happenstance; Miss Ryan might have mistaken his mother for an old memory of a similar-looking woman in a faded photograph.

The housekeeper led them to a paneled study. Though it bore the comforts of a fire, the austere brown furnishings seemed as cold and harsh as the bearded gentleman who appraised them from a mahogany chair. He closed his book but didn't rise. Strong in build despite his advanced years, he reminded Peter of a polar bear, with his snow-white hair and pale skin.

"You wished to see me?" Mr. Underhill's greeting lacked any welcome.

"I was told you might be able to help me," Peter rasped, and he cleared his throat. "Sixteen years ago I lost my mother when the *Titanic* foundered; I think you might know her."

"Indeed?" Mr. Underhill's tone left no doubt that he thought such a possibility utter nonsense.

Peter had come too far to back down now. He opened the locket and held it out to the man. Mr. Underhill didn't accept it, giving only the barest and most indifferent of glances to the treasured oval.

"I've never seen this woman."

"Perhaps you're mistaken; please look again." Peter worked to hide his annoyance.

"I told you I don't know her. Now if you would be so good as to leave my home, my housekeeper will show you the door."

Peter sensed something amiss, judging by the man's uncooperative attitude alone; Missy also looked at the man askance, confusion on her face. Other than demand Mr. Underhill take a long look at the photo, which Peter had no intention of doing, he had no recourse but to do as the man wished and leave.

"Please, sir," Missy said, surprising Peter. "We're not asking for a lot. Just for you to take a good look at the photograph."

"What is it you hope to gain?" Mr. Underhill changed his tactic, first looking at Missy, then at Peter. "You have come, perhaps, with the claim of being a long-lost relation? Don't bother. We had one son, and he's dead. He had no child, and we have no grandson."

"I don't recall making mention of any such possibility. I thank you for your time." Peter's words came clipped, and he signaled to Missy that they should go.

Once out of the oppressive room, Peter didn't draw a breath of relief until they were outside. Too many uncertainties clamored inside his mind for him to make normal conversation, though he sensed Missy's frequent glances his way.

They'd gone about fifty feet down the sidewalk when a slight, feminine voice called for them to stop. Peter turned to see a petite woman dressed in a fine, black lace dress, her silver hair upswept. She pressed a hand to her heart and walked closer, eyeing Peter.

"May I see that locket?"

Her words came out in mere breaths, as if she'd rushed to catch up with them. She continued staring at Peter as he handed her the locket, then looked down at it. She stared at the oval a long time, and Peter observed her carefully. A number of emotions flitted across her face, but he had difficulty classifying any of them.

"Did you know her?" he asked quietly.

She didn't answer right away, but after a moment, she looked up. "No, I never knew her." What looked like regret filled her green eyes as she placed the locket into his palm. "I'm so sorry." Her words seemed more than a courtesy. She clasped his hand with her other one in sympathy, her strong grip surprising Peter.

"Millicent?"

She glanced over her shoulder toward the house. "I must

go. I hope you find what you're looking for. You seem like such a nice young man. Perhaps—"

"Millicent!"

All of them looked toward the porch. Mr. Underhill moved through the door, his stance forbidding.

"I must go." She gave Peter one last glance. "Good-bye."

Peter stared after her. Once she reached the steps, Mr. Underhill took hold of her arm, glared at Peter one final time, then turned with the woman into the house.

"What do you make of that?" Missy echoed Peter's thoughts.

"Peculiar, to say the least." Peter forced the words through a tight throat. "Her actions seemed almost guilt-ridden."

"You think you're related, don't you? That they're your grandparents."

He blew out a weary breath steeped in frustration. "I don't know what to think. Sometimes, I'm almost sorry I started this venture."

"Well, at least you can put this part of your quest behind you." Missy's words did little to comfort, though he smiled in gratitude for her attempt.

"Perhaps it's time to abandon the entire hunt."

She didn't respond immediately. "Whatever you decide, you can be grateful for one thing, Peter."

"Oh, what's that?"

"You might be a different man today had you been raised by the Underhills. A man not in possession of so many admirable qualities."

Her words struck a chord of truth within him, but he centered on her last words. "You think I have admirable qualities?"

A flush of pink tinted her face. "Yes. Of course." She averted her gaze to the mansion. "And my praise doesn't come easily; I can't say the same about many men."

"Let's walk." Wanting to learn more about her, he broached a new subject as they retraced their steps. "Did you know your father?"

She shook her head. "He died when I was two. I only have his name to remember him by; I don't even possess a picture like you have of your mother." Sadness tinged her voice, but she threw him a tepid smile. "The men of my mother's acquaintance could hardly be described as admirable. Even Maria's brother—the don—wasn't without his vices. He had a hot temper, though I suppose one couldn't really blame him since he had to deal with my mother every day. I later learned we were sailing on the *Titanic* because he had sent her home to New York and away from Spain. He never came to the States any time after that." Her voice grew vague; then she suddenly turned to him.

"Oh—something I've wanted to ask, but I kept forgetting. The woman who raised you, you said her name was Annabelle. Is that right?" At his nod, wonder filled her eyes. "Remember when I said that I invited a woman to my birthday party on the *Titanic?* Her name was Annabelle; I remember because I named my doll after her. She was different than the other adults on the ship; she talked to me like I was important. Do you think my Annabelle could be the same person as your mother?"

"From your description, there's a very good chance they could be the same. Annabelle treats everyone with the same measure of kindness, whether they are a servant or a lady. When I was in the infirmary on the *Carpathia,* she came to see me though we were strangers, and she held me while I cried. Since that night, she's helped to fill in the gap left in my life, she and Lawrence both."

"Peter, if those people *are* your grandparents, I doubt they would have given you half the love and support your adoptive parents gave you and that you needed so badly, considering all the losses you suffered." Her tone grew tentative. "It's almost as though God had a hand in placing you with the right people."

"Thank you, Missy. That helps to take away some of the

sting of my father's rejection. And the Underhills'."

She gave a brief nod. "So, where do we go from here? Since you believe you found them, do you still want to visit the others on the list?"

"Yes, I suppose so. I still have too many unanswered questions, and if I don't seek out those people, I'll never know if one of them might have held a key to any of them. Queens adjoins Long Island, correct?" At her nod, he continued, "Then I imagine we should try there next."

ten

Queens proved to be a disappointment. Mr. Jack Frohmann had moved to New Jersey the previous month, and his neighbor had no forwarding address. Melissa noticed Peter worked hard to bury his disappointment and keep the cheerful outlook that she'd helped him rediscover at the lake.

That had been the first time she'd ever seen him so discouraged and prepared to give up. Under the circumstances she couldn't blame him, and if Mr. Underhill hadn't unnerved her so badly, she might have worked up enough courage to tell him exactly what she thought of his belittling attitude toward Peter. She'd wanted to shake Mrs. Underhill, to make her admit to Peter what he so needed to hear to help him fit that absent link onto the chain of his life. Like Peter, Melissa felt almost certain the Underhills were his grandparents, judging by their peculiar behavior alone.

"Rather than visit Mr. Harper, the last person on the list, I think I'd prefer to spend the rest of the day visiting memorials. Would you care to come along?"

"Of course."

Melissa didn't understand why he should suddenly feel the need to ask, nor did she question why she agreed so readily. Any time spent with Peter she considered a gift, and she realized she was fast coming to care for him. She wanted so badly for him to succeed in his quest, and when he ran up against a brick wall, she felt his discouragement and pain as if they were her own.

They returned to Manhattan to visit the memorials erected to those outstanding passengers of the *Titanic*. First they shared a late lunch at a small café; then they viewed the

Titanic Memorial Lighthouse, which sat perched atop the roof of the Seaman's Institute, where the crew's survivors had stayed during their recovery. A man passing by them on the street stopped to watch and told them that at the stroke of noon every day, a ball at the top of the imitation lighthouse dropped down to signal the hour to boats in the harbor.

The Wireless Operators Memorial in Battery Park faced the inner harbor and the Statue of Liberty. Inscribed with the names of men, the granite stone had been erected as a commemoration to their heroism and their futile but courageous efforts to make contact with a ship closer than the *Carpathia*. Next, Melissa and Peter traveled to a V-shaped park at Broadway and 106th Street, where the statue of a graceful lady reclined near a reflecting pool, her head propped on one hand, her other hand framing her cheek in a winsome manner. The memorial plaque paid homage to Isidor and Ida Straus. Melissa stroked the folds of the statue's gown, thinking about the former owners of Macy's and the words of the shoe clerk, Mr. Delaney. Ida Straus had given up her seat in a lifeboat, claiming she'd lived fifty years with her husband and would not leave him.

Awed by such devotion, Melissa felt a tear slip from her eye. It would take a very special man to make a woman want to sacrifice her life just to remain by his side for what could only amount to minutes for both of them. Without conscious thought, Melissa's glance lifted to Peter.

He looked at her at the same time, and she felt her face warm.

"These people had a trait you don't often see," he said.

"What's that?"

"The courage to die, to face death with equanimity."

She nodded. "They had more than that, I think. They had each others' love to support them in their crisis; without that love, I wonder if they could have been so strong."

His admiring gaze only added to the fire in her cheeks.

Taking a taxicab to Central Park, they found upon one wall

another memorial in honor of William T. Stead, a British journalist.

"The original is on the Thames in London," Peter said. "I've seen it as well. See there at the bottom—" He pointed to a figurine of a medieval knight on the left corner and one in long robes in the opposite corner. "Those two statuettes symbolize courage and charity, two attributes that were demonstrated by many that night."

Melissa studied the small statues.

"Mr. Stead wrote of passenger-liner accidents in the years before the *Titanic;* how ironic that he experienced all of what he wrote but didn't live to tell about it."

Melissa shuddered; so many ironies and coincidences seemed connected with that night and with Peter's life now. On Long Island, she hadn't really thought about it, but now she found it amazing that Miss Ryan had happened to be at the hotel just when Peter showed Mrs. Arbunckle the locket, and that she'd been a maid at the Underhills, though the venture to their mansion hadn't brought about much success.

Melissa saw a pattern, and the consistencies gave her pause. Maybe Maria was right and God in His heaven did care enough to direct the everyday course of His children on earth. Perhaps He stood at the helm of Peter's quest even now, without either of them realizing it.

"Missy?"

The concern in Peter's tone made her lift her head.

"Are you still with me?" When she only stared, he explained, "You seem so far away."

She preferred not to speak of what had been on her heart. Not yet. Not until she had time to dwell on it further. "Tell me about London, Peter. About England. I was too young to remember much of the short time we were there."

"What do you wish to know?"

"Everything. Does the king always wear his crown?"

He laughed as though delighted, and Melissa smiled,

realizing how silly that sounded. "I meant when he travels in public, of course."

"On the occasions I have seen him, he did wear it, yes. I cannot account for any other times." He moved closer and took gentle hold of her arm. "Let's find a place to sit down, shall we? Then I'll satisfy your curiosities about England to your heart's content."

"You want to sit here?" Melissa looked at the trees around them.

"Why not? It is a park. And surely where there is a park, there's also a bench."

She refrained from telling him that Central Park was also a hangout for thieves and bums. After witnessing him fire the rifle, she had the feeling he could take care of them both. At first, it had made her uneasy to witness his prowess with the weapon; the man was a sharpshooter, no mistake about it. Guns made her nervous, but perhaps it was really Guido and his mob that unsettled her.

They found a bench on which to rest, and Peter filled her mind and heart with tales of the beauty of his homeland. She could almost experience the relics of castles and view the morning mist breaking up along the glens and moors, could almost feel the ancient mystery of the land where kings and queens resided. And she envisioned knights of old who fought in tournaments and rescued their ladies fair.

She decided that, one day, she would visit Great Britain. She didn't know how she could accomplish such a feat, but she wanted to know more about the land from which this amazing man came, wanted to know more about him.

After her frightening experience on that April Sunday of 1912, when the *Titanic* had sunk below the depths of the icy sea, New York City had become the cradle which had nurtured the child Melissa had been. The city had taught her, opening her eyes to some harsh realities, and it also had helped her to mature. But she'd had enough of the gangsters and crime that had increased since Prohibition started, and she wanted an end to that life. She wanted to experience peace.

As though Peter read her mind, he broke off from his tale concerning his visit to Windsor Castle, his expression sincere. "You should come to visit England; I think you would love it there. And of course, you would be our guest."

She smiled. "I can think of nothing I'd like better."

❧

Peter felt certain he had read more into Missy's words than what she'd meant. Since that afternoon when she spoke of her desire to visit England, Peter had replayed the entire conversation in his mind. Dreams of Missy filled his sleep, and when he awoke, she was his first thought. A glance at his pocket watch showed him he must hurry, and he dressed quickly and ate breakfast in a hotel restaurant.

His list had narrowed down to one last passenger he wanted to question. First, however, he planned to visit the White Star offices the moment they opened and attempt once again to get a look at the passenger list. In Liverpool, the secretary had been uncooperative in locating the copy used in the British hearings, and when pressed, the man had claimed he was unable to locate it; Peter hoped his efforts to obtain the list from the American hearings would be rewarded.

Mr. Fromby's secretary, Mrs. Little, was as intimidating as Roger had painted her to be. She looked up at Peter suspiciously over the edges of her half-moon glasses. "May I help you?"

Her tone seemed contrary to the greeting, as if she'd rather kick him back out the door he'd just entered. Peter tipped his hat and gave her his most charming smile. The frost in her eyes melted a fraction.

"I was here last week. Your janitor, Roger, told me that you might be of some assistance to me. I seek the passenger list belonging to the *Titanic*, especially those passengers in first and second class." Quickly he produced the locket and opened it, forestalling a negative response. "This was my mother. She died that night and left me with a mystery to solve. I wish only to look at the names to see if I'm able to locate a familiar one."

As the woman surveyed the locket and Peter for what seemed an eternity, Peter's disappointment rose. At last she spoke.

"Roger told me about your visit. He also spoke with Mr. Fromby, who's away on business at the moment. Mr. Fromby consulted with his associates, and they've agreed to grant your request. If you'll wait right here, I'll return presently."

Peter could only stare in surprise that she'd given him the permission he'd sought. He'd been ready to engage in polite warfare and could barely grasp that the surrender had come without any need to parley.

She soon returned and handed him a sheaf of papers. Peter took the thin stack and stared at it, disbelief mingling with an odd sense of profound sentiment. In his hands were the names of many; names once linked to the faces of people young and old, wealthy and poor, all who shared two common traits: Each of these passengers once possessed individual hopes and dreams. And each one of them as a group had shared the fear and loss that tragic night.

"You can sit over there in that chair." As if she understood his hesitation, Mrs. Little's words came tentatively, breaking into Peter's thoughts.

Peter nodded his thanks. Once seated, he turned to the surnames beginning with the letter F. Just as his father had said, he found no woman by the name of Franklin listed among the passengers, though a man's name was there. Had Peter's memory been faulty? He'd forgotten so much; what if he'd misunderstood the name the few times he'd heard it, as well? Not many children at the age of seven possessed knowledge of their mother's first name or even their surname. He'd never been addressed by his surname at that age—not that he could remember.

His hand began to shake as he ran his index finger down

the columns. Fillbrook. . .Flegenheim. . .Flynn. . .Fortune. . .
Fox. . Franklin, Mr. . .Funk. . . Fynney. Nothing. He closed his
eyes and drew a deep breath, thinking. As if some unknown
force directed him, he felt compelled to flip back a page to the
beginning of the list of surnames beginning with F and search
there. Duran. . .Eitmeiler. . .Enanader. . .Fahlstrom. . .

His focus halted on the next name, and a sense of unreality
pervaded his soul, even while truth whispered to his heart:

Farlan, Miss Lily
Farlan, Master Peter W.

Tears clouded his eyes, and the words swam before him.
Gently, he brushed his fingertip over the fine black print.

His mother's name was Lily.

Despite what this proved—that she'd never married, and he
was indeed nameless—the little boy who'd never had the chance
to say good-bye reached out now to cling to this snippet of his
mother's existence. In so doing, the memory of being held in her
arms comforted him, and he knew if he possessed nothing else,
he once had had his mother's love.

eleven

The moment Melissa saw Peter enter the restaurant, she knew something of great magnitude had occurred. Bittersweet knowledge filled his blue eyes, and his smile seemed to falter.

"Peter, what's wrong?"

"My last name was *Farlan*, not *Franklin*."

She let out a soft sigh in understanding. "You saw the list? You went to the White Star offices this morning?"

He nodded. "My mother never married; it was as I thought all along. I have no legitimate father."

Melissa held a stunned breath—stunned because of the revelation that catapulted through her head with his admission. With this new turn of events, Claire would never accept him as a prospective husband. Now that he knew the truth, Peter could be free, if he so chose. But what of his heart? Would it forever be bound to the woman who'd denied it?

"Such things don't matter," she said to cover the strength of her emotions at the worry that all his searching would come to nothing if he didn't learn to let go of Claire. "It doesn't make you any more or less the man you are, the remarkable man you've become."

His smile was tinged with both gratitude and regret. "With you as my champion, things don't seem quite so bleak."

"Good." She moved to collect her coat from the chair. "Do you still intend to visit Mr. Harper?"

"I see no reason to do so. I know the truth of who I am now."

She didn't like the defeated tone that underscored his words; this attitude was so unlike him. "Since he's the last one on the list, I say we should go. His home is closer than the others were; we can at least go there and see what he has to add, if anything."

"The day I first met you, I went to see him but received no answer to my knock. I tried again on my way from the hotel a few days ago."

"That doesn't mean he's not home now."

"All right, Missy." His words were resigned. "We'll try."

"Don't give up yet, Peter. God didn't bring you across an entire ocean to abandon you when you need Him most."

He regarded her with surprise. "I thought you didn't believe in guidance from a higher source."

"I said I wasn't sure what to believe. But the more I think on this, the more inclined I am to think a divine hand must have arranged the times and places: first your meeting on the ship with that steward who suggested our restaurant, then your meeting with Roger who just happened to remember all those people and gave you a list of where to find them. True, not every tip paid off, but then again, we don't know what all might have been set in motion. Maybe God intended that we be there for them. Like that woman at the movie theater, maybe she needed the reminder of the tragedy so she could finally release any unhealthy grief she still suffered. Who knows?" She shrugged.

Peter stared at her as if he'd never seen her before.

"I know this all sounds a bit farfetched, but I just can't let go of the idea. Too much has happened to chalk it up to mere coincidence. Remember the message at the service last Sunday? About how God desires to give His children every good thing, but sometimes He waits to act so that more people can receive the blessing?" At Peter's nod, she went on. "Maybe that's what's happening now, Peter. God waited to act, to inspire you to go on this quest so He could bring this all together in His way and His time, so that many could benefit and not just one."

Her words tumbled out in her excitement, but she hadn't been able to get the idea out of her mind since the revelation first hit her. "And what's more, I don't think you're supposed to quit your search until you fit the last piece in place. Does that make any sense, or do I sound completely batty?"

At this, he laughed, the delight in his voice genuine. Melissa could have cheered to hear him sound at ease again.

"Actually, Missy, I believe it makes a great deal of sense. My mother Annabelle raised me to believe in God's guidance, though as I've mentioned before, I've questioned its existence. During some of those times, she gave as an example the story of how she believed He had helped her to locate a little girl who went missing that night. The girl had run back to her cabin to hide beneath her bed, and Mother found her."

Missy smiled through the tears that sprang to her eyes. "Peter, *I* was that girl."

"You, Missy?"

She nodded, remembering. "I was so scared. Maria dragged me out of the cabin, and before we reached the top deck, I realized I didn't have one of my dolls. I pulled away from her and ran back. Everything was falling apart everywhere. Water had risen to the lower levels, lights exploded all around me, and sparks flew, things crashed and broke apart—people were screaming, some were hurt and bleeding. It was horrible; I was so frightened. I found our cabin—Maria had left the door open—and I crawled underneath the bed to hide. Annabelle found me there. When I was old enough to understand, I realized she saved my life. I never forgot that—or her."

"And Lawrence saved mine." Peter looked at her in wonder and slowly shook his head. "It would seem God has woven our lives together almost from the start, in more ways than one and without either of us knowing about it. If I had any doubts regarding the possibility of God's guidance before this, the truth of His intervention is becoming more difficult to counter with cold logic."

Melissa had thought nothing more could stun her; she was wrong. "It's almost as if He made a bridge across the sea to bring you here." *And to bring us together,* she finished silently. For now she admitted what she'd been afraid to face before: she had come to love Peter.

As they continued to gaze at one another, she sensed the fragile bond that linked them strengthen. And though he made no move toward her, in Melissa's heart, she felt as if they'd connected.

&

At Jacob Harper's residence, a woman in her thirties answered the door. Her face looked haggard; her eyes kind. Peter introduced himself and explained his mission.

"I'm so sorry," she said. "I'm Maude Harper; Jacob Harper was my father. He died a few weeks ago."

"May I offer my condolences? And please, forgive me for troubling you." Discomfited, Peter took Missy by the arm and moved to go.

"No. Wait." Maude motioned they should step inside. "It's all right. Really. And please excuse the disorder. I've been boxing up his possessions; the lease is up, you see, and I have to move everything out of here or risk losing it. He was such a packrat." Her laugh was shallow and choked, a failed attempt at lightness.

Peter nodded, yet couldn't help but notice Miss Harper's red-rimmed eyes. He felt uneasy bothering the woman at such a difficult time, even though she'd invited them inside.

"I can return another time," he said.

"I'm afraid there won't be another time. I'll be moving to Connecticut to stay with my aunt. Please, it's all right. I want to show you something."

Curious despite himself, he acquiesced, and the woman excused herself.

Peter shared a look with Missy and saw reflected in her eyes the same sympathetic disquiet. The woman soon returned, turning a slim book over in her hands and peering at its black and gold binding.

"Father always wanted to be a novelist; he was constantly

gathering tidbits of useless information to create characters he planned to use someday. He did the same on the *Titanic*." She handed Peter the book. Opening it, he noted that a man's strong handwriting filled the pages. "He carried this in his coat pocket all the time, and that night was no different. He was one of the lucky few who found a lifeboat. The officers who loaded those earlier boats didn't know better, I suppose. They allowed men on too, but only on that side of the ship.

"Later, Father said he felt guilty for taking what could have been a woman's seat—very few knew there weren't enough lifeboats at the time—and though this may sound selfish, I'm glad he did get off the ship. I don't think I could have survived losing him, too. I had just lost my mother the previous year," she explained.

"All that aside. . ." She looked down at the book Peter held. "He kept that, always saying he planned to write a story of what those days were like. He never did; I just don't think he had the heart to do so."

Peter nodded, thinking about all the sacrifices of that night. He closed the book and held it out to her, but she made no move to take it.

"I want you to have it. It won't do me any good. There's already so much I have to remember him by, and I probably won't be able to keep half of his possessions. Please," she stressed when Peter hesitated. "I think he would've wanted you to have it; if you knew my father, you'd know it would have cheered him to think his scribblings could bring about some good. That's what he wanted to do, you see. Inspire people and make them think. He wanted to be a writer, to reach the people." She gave a rueful laugh. "Though I'm afraid he was somewhat scatterbrained with the way he recorded the information. Still, if you can make sense of his meanderings, they might help you find the answers you lack."

Moved, Peter pocketed the journal and clasped her hand with both of his. "Thank you. Your gift is most appreciated."

Once they were on the sidewalk, Missy turned to him. "May I see it?"

"Of course. Let's sit down first." They entered nearby Central Park, and he handed her the book. She flipped through the first few pages. "He's dated everything, showing the place and time of meeting and a physical and character description of the passengers. Amazing. Listen to this: 'Although many on board desire little to do with the magnanimous Mrs. J. J. Brown, whose mouth one finds can be considered almost as wide as her heart, I would warrant that a more noble woman could not be found on the ship.' It goes on to give a physical description of her—hair brassy red, eyes blue. . . .'" Missy looked up and froze, then glanced away.

"Perhaps we should return to the restaurant. I find that I'm suddenly hungry." She stood.

Confused, Peter also stood while casting a glance in the direction Missy had looked. Two men stood conversing with one another. Upon closer appraisal, Peter recognized them as restaurant patrons to whom Tony had spoken on the first night Peter heard Missy sing. Tony had left Peter's table quite abruptly to speak with the men.

"Who are they?" Peter noticed one of the men glance their way.

"Don't look at them," she whispered, staring in another direction. "Just walk with me and pretend you didn't see them. They're Guido's men."

"Will they cause trouble?"

"From past experience, they'll report to Guido that they saw me here. You have nothing to worry about."

"I'm not worried for myself, Missy. I'm concerned for you."

"Other than grab me and run, they wouldn't do anything, and I'm sure they wouldn't even do that. They only follow their boss's orders. I'm not sure they were even following me; it might just be dumb bad luck we ended up where they are, but I know they've seen me now."

Clenching his jaw, Peter put his hand to the small of Missy's back and guided her out of the park and away from their view.

He wanted answers to the mystery of Guido, and he felt that her uncle Tony was the place to start.

twelve

Once Missy left to prepare for the restaurant's evening customers, Peter sought out Tony. Maria sent Peter to a back office, where he found the man sitting at a desk, his head clutched in his hands.

"Mr. Marelli?"

The man straightened, eyeing Peter with surprise. He smiled nervously to cover his earlier agitation. "Please, call me Tony."

"Very well. Tony." Peter motioned to the other chair. "May I?"

"Of course." If Tony was curious as to the reason for Peter's visit, he didn't show it.

Peter took a seat. "I wish to know more about this man, Guido Piccoli."

Wariness glinted in Tony's eyes, and he gave an indifferent shrug. "He is one of my customers."

"A dangerous customer who's formed an attachment to Missy, one she clearly doesn't return. What I wish to know— is Missy in any real danger?"

Tony's act of ignorance slipped. He shut his eyes and hung his head. "The Piccolis get what they want. Who's to say what will happen with them always calling the shots?"

Peter felt alarmed at the man's obvious dismissal of the situation. "Can't you do something to stop his harassment? Alert the authorities?"

Tony let out a humorless laugh. "Vittorio's family is untouchable. They have connections with those who run most of New York, and they have informers—spies—everywhere."

Recalling Tony's actions that first night and how he rushed to the table to speak with the two men, Peter asked quietly,

"How did you get involved with them, Tony?"

Tony looked up, surprised. A second look of resignation crossed his dark features. "Do not tell Maria. My father was indebted to them, and when I first started this restaurant, Guido helped, though I did not ask for his help. Now he feels I am indebted to him for life. It is the way with these people. They give small favors, then expect much in return."

"And now Vittorio's nephew wants Missy for his bride."

"The family does not marry outside of their own kind." Pained disgust clipped Tony's words.

"Then why. . ." Understanding rang clear in his mind, and Peter's jaw hardened. "We cannot let that man get hold of her, Tony. I don't want her to travel anywhere in the city alone; you or I or Lucio must be with her at all times. Guido's men were at Central Park today. Missy claimed it was all coincidence, but I'm not certain it was."

Tony dropped his head into his hands. "Maria would never forgive me if something happened to Melissa."

Peter hesitated. "She told me you own a handgun. I'd like to carry it for her protection."

"Of course. It was my father's, so it is somewhat old."

"Anything is better than nothing."

Tony regarded him steadily. "You love her."

Said aloud, the words didn't shock Peter as much as he thought they would. He'd played them over and over in his mind while in his hotel room. "Yes, I love her."

Tony nodded. "This is good. You are a strong man and will be good for Melissa. She's been hurt—in her feelings—by men all her life. You are not one of them. She loves you, too." Tony gave a quick nod of emphasis.

"She told you that?" Peter could barely frame the words.

"No, I see it. In her eyes." Tony's smile was sad. "She will be missed, but it is good for her to go from this place. You will take her back with you? To England?" He raised his thick brows.

Peter wasn't exactly sure what he'd planned, but this conversation had gotten entirely out of hand. Yes, he'd pondered a future with Missy, but he didn't want to share those thoughts with her uncle. Not yet. "Missy might not want to leave New York," he said in a weak attempt to satisfy the man's curiosity when Tony continued to stare as if awaiting an answer.

"She will want to go."

Later at his hotel, Peter couldn't rest. Tony's words played a continuously in his mind. He read a few pages from Mr. Harper's notebook, but his thoughts wandered. The bold, sloppy handwriting became harder to decipher, and Peter felt a headache coming on. Deciding he needed air, he took a walk along the wharf and stared out to sea.

"Are you planning to throw yourself in, or wondering how to bail yourself out?"

At the smooth words delivered with a trace of French accent, Peter swivelled to stare at the man who'd come up behind him. Gray streaked his fair hair, and lines crisscrossed his sharp features, but his eyes seemed kind.

"Pardon?"

The man nodded toward the ocean. "You look as if you carry a millstone around your neck."

"I have a lot on my mind."

"Tell me to mind my own business if you'd prefer, but I've found it sometimes helps to talk with a stranger. You never need see the person again so don't have to fear what they think of you. I run a soup kitchen not far from the wharf. Why not come with me and enjoy a bowl?"

"I wouldn't wish to take away food from those in true need of it."

The Frenchman laughed. "Believe me, we cook up plenty. And it's good too; my wife knows her spices well."

Peter nodded, uncertain if it was the stranger's friendly attitude or his own need to confide in another individual that led him to accept the invitation.

The soup kitchen appeared little more than a hovel, but the air simmered with the spicy aroma of soup. The handful of dockworkers in the place seemed happy.

While he ate the clam chowder, which was every bit as good as the man claimed, Peter told his story from the beginning, without naming any names but Guido's. His host listened intently, his blue eyes sparking with surprise when Peter spoke of sailing on the *Titanic* and of running away from gangsters.

"That is quite a story," his host said after a long moment. "May I share a piece of advice?"

"Of course."

"Do not second-guess Guido and his bunch. I've had many dealings with men such as these. For all their foolishness, they are smart and will act when you least expect them to. I know this from experience. Before accepting Christ, I was one of them. A dangerous criminal, a lowlife of the worst sort. I worked for Vittorio at one point in my life."

Peter found such a thing hard to believe, but his host nodded, his eyes solemn.

"*Oui.* It is true. Ironically, the woman I hurt the most was also the one who helped me the most. She taught me about absolute forgiveness, and her friend showed me an act of undeserved kindness. It was in jail that I grew to understand both, and later I found true freedom."

A towheaded boy ran up to their table and spoke quickly in French; the man answered him, then turned to Peter.

"I apologize. I must leave you. My wife needs me." He shrugged in a blithe manner, his eyes twinkling in amusement. "Probably to open a jar. I will pray that God gives you all the guidance you need in this matter."

As the child led the man away by the hand, Peter realized he'd never even thought to ask his host's name.

When Peter returned to his hotel, the clerk at the front desk stopped him.

"Mr. Caldwell, while you were out, a woman rang for you. She left a message." From a slot he withdrew a note and handed it to Peter.

Certain it must be from Missy, he tried to hide his alarm. She'd never contacted him at his hotel before tonight, and he worried that the threat of Guido might have been what prompted the call.

In the elevator, he unfolded the note and read:

> *Please meet me at the Japanese Teahouse in Manhattan tomorrow at noon. I have something I would like to share with you.*
>
> *Respectfully yours,*
> *Mrs. Lorne Underhill*

thirteen

Melissa noticed Peter bounce the crown of his hat against his leg as they stood outside the painted screen enclosing the room and waited for the oriental woman in the red kimono to slide the door along its track. Smiling, she motioned they were to take off their shoes first.

Melissa felt Peter's shock and saw him jerk back when the woman knelt as if she would do it for him. "It's all right," Melissa said to the waitress. "I'll take care of it."

The woman bowed, as she'd done often since they'd met at the front of the Japanese restaurant. She gave Peter an uncertain look before gracefully scurrying away.

Missy knelt before Peter.

"Missy, no. Don't."

Anxious dread laced his voice, but she sensed he wouldn't be able to do this task and keep his balance, since no chairs were in the vicinity on which to sit. "She won't be looking at your feet," she whispered. Before he could argue further, she untied and slipped off his shoe, then did the same with the other one. Her heart clenched at the sight of his misshapen sock, but she guarded her pity well as she stood and slipped out of her own black pumps, depositing them next to his shoes. "What is it you British like to say? Pip pip, keep a stiff upper lip, and all that?"

He rewarded her with a low laugh. The tenderness softening his eyes made her wish for a moment that Mrs. Underhill wasn't on the other side of the screen. He slid the door open for Melissa to precede him.

Within the screened area, a circular table sat low to the floor, pillows of all colors piled around it. Mrs. Underhill sat on one of them, looking decidedly uncomfortable with her legs tucked up close to her body and the hem of her black skirt pulled tight to cover every inch of her stockings. Melissa had the feeling her choice of a meeting place stemmed from the need for discretion rather than the desire for cuisine.

After stiff greetings all around, Peter relied on his cane to lower himself to a sitting position and laid his hat on another pillow. Melissa sank to the pillow beside him, and both stared at Mrs. Underhill across the table.

Such wistfulness touched her expression as she stared at Peter that it took Melissa's breath away.

"You have your father's eyes," she said at last. "I can see him inside you."

The Japanese woman returned at that moment, bearing a platter with a variety of small dishes and postponing any reply as she gracefully laid each one in its spot on the table. An electric tension shivered in the air, and Melissa noted the stunned look on Peter's face. They had guessed his lineage, but hearing they'd been correct still brought surprise.

Once the waitress left with more bows and smiles and closed the door behind her, Peter leaned forward.

"Why?"

The pained fury encased in that one soft syllable left no doubt as to his meaning. Mrs. Underhill bowed her head a moment before looking at Peter again.

"My husband is a very harsh man. Clayton—your father—loved Lily, but my husband wouldn't budge in his decision. He had his own plans for our son, and they didn't include marriage to a foreigner. But Clayton opposed him and married your mother, bringing her with him to America."

Peter inhaled a swift lungful of air. "They were married?"

"For a time." Mrs. Underhill studied her blue-veined hands clasped on the table. "My husband deceived Lily, even staging a scene that made Clayton appear unfaithful, and she left your father, returning to England. Clayton never got over her and despised his father more with each passing year. But one thing frightened him more than losing your mother; he feared poverty, and he knew my husband would cut him out of the will should he flee to England."

She released a sigh of sad resignation. "Later, I learned Lily had been pregnant when she left, and they had been communicating for years; a friend of Clayton's acted as a go-between, and the letters were mailed to his bungalow. On the night before the *Carpathia* pulled in to port, Clayton admitted the truth and told me Lily was coming to him with their child. He was so fearful that you both might not have survived the sinking of the *Titanic* and that he was too late. I never was so proud of him as when he vowed that he would do all he must to make a living for the two of you, and that he would have his family with him again. That was the night my son grew up.

Unfortunately, my husband overheard his declaration, and they had a horrible row. Clayton stormed out of the house, and that was the last I ever saw him."

She fumbled for a handkerchief from her purse and pressed the bunched cloth against her eyes. Melissa felt her own eyes water. The food sat forgotten as they each became lost in their thoughts.

Mrs. Underhill cleared her throat and pulled a wrapped bundle from her handbag, handing it across the table to Peter. "These are all the letters your mother wrote to your father." She reached into her bag again. "And this is their picture. He kept it on his bureau. They're yours now."

Peter took the framed oval, the size of his hand, and stared at it without comment. Melissa leaned in to look, struck by the resemblance Peter bore to the man in the photograph. The woman most definitely was his mother; she even wore the same dress she had for the picture contained in the locket, and Melissa wondered if the daguerreotypes had been taken the same day.

"Peter. . ."

The yearning in the woman's voice had him lift his gaze.

"I wanted you, wanted to find you. But my husband. . ." Tears filled her eyes again, and she cut off her words, shaking her head in despair.

"I understand." He gave her a slight smile of assurance, but Melissa knew him well enough to sense its stiffness.

"Do you? I hope you really do and you're not just saying that to make me feel better. I don't deserve it, but I knew I wouldn't be able to sleep tonight if I didn't meet with you. I had to see you once more. Clayton would have wanted you to know the truth." She stood suddenly. "I must get back before I'm missed. And please, don't think too harshly of us. Your grandfather's had a hard life; he wasn't always a steel tycoon, and I. . .well, I've never had enough courage to stand up to him and tell him he was wrong, to insist we search for you. Clayton's death devastated me, and I barely spoke to anyone for weeks. But I did want you, so very much." Her words thickened, and she pressed the handkerchief to her mouth, hurrying from the screened room without another word.

Peter stared at the plate in front of him.

"Peter?" Concerned, Melissa laid a hand on his sleeve.

"I'm all right. Actually, I feel sorrier for her than I do for myself."

"I know what you mean. And I find myself more grateful than ever that you weren't raised in that household." Melissa did sympathize with the woman and her plight yet couldn't help but feel a twinge of righteous indignation on Peter's behalf. "Well. . ." She looked toward the untouched food. "Should we eat as long as we're here?"

"You can eat if you'd like. I'm not all that hungry."

"Neither am I."

His eyes met hers. "Thank you for coming with me today, for supporting me. I didn't want to do this alone."

"Hey, we're a team, remember? I'm with you every step of the way." Her light response belied the rapid beating of her heart. They sat close, and almost without her realizing it, the atmosphere changed. She looked deeply into his eyes, feeling she could drown there, then down to his lips, hoping he would try to kiss her again.

Instead he looked away and cleared his throat, breaking the moment. "We should go." He struggled to use his cane to help himself up.

"Here, let me. Sitting on the floor doesn't make it easy to rise gracefully." She laughed as her own scramble to her feet grew awkward.

She grasped his hand with both of hers and pulled hard, while he relied on her support to get a decent footing. But her silk stockings slid on the floor, and she couldn't maintain a good foothold. Suddenly, she found herself pulled down and sprawled on top of him.

Startled, they stared into each other's eyes.

"I'm sorry," she breathed. "Did I hurt you?"

"Missy, you couldn't hurt me if you tried." Peter's gaze grew serious. "Unless, of course, you told me to go away and never come back. Now that. . .that would hurt me."

She inhaled softly at his candid words. "Put your mind at rest then, because that's never going to happen. Haven't you figured out yet that I've completely fallen for you?"

They moved toward one another at the same time. Their lips met, and Missy's heart sang with its first note of love.

The sound of the door sliding on its track, followed by a nervous titter of laughter, broke them apart. They both turned their heads toward the door, where the Japanese woman laughed delicately behind her fingertips.

"So sorry," she said. "I come back soon." She left, sliding the door closed again.

Peter groaned. "Before whatever reputation you have left is hopelessly tarnished by the gossipmongers, I think it wise for us to get up off this floor. I have a feeling we've just become the new topic of conversation."

She laughed and crawled off of him. When she held out her hand again, he shook his head, instead using both his cane and the table to stand.

"Chicken," she teased.

"No." He struggled to his feet. When he almost lost his balance, she put out her arm to aid him, and he turned to her, his eyes steady. "I simply know my limits."

His words teased, but his eyes didn't, and she felt a shiver of pleasurable warmth rush through her.

"Peter, what just happened between us?"

He studied her as if now cautious. "What do you think happened?"

"I think. . . ." She bit her lower lip. "I think I just told you how I feel about you, but I'm still uncertain where you stand."

"Where I stand?"

"How you feel about me." Embarrassment warmed her face. "I'm new at this sort of thing, so if I sound naive, it's because I am."

At her second outburst of nervous laughter, his expression grew serious. "How I feel about you. . ."

She swallowed hard as he drew closer.

"I cannot sleep for thinking of you. Though I spend all my days with you, I find it's not enough. I take every opportunity to travel to your restaurant, foregoing a marvelous eatery within my own hotel, just to see your face and hear your voice each night." With each sentence he spoke, her eyes widened farther, but he didn't stop there. "The thought of returning to England without you is unbearable, and I've found myself trying to think up excuses to stay in New York a little while longer now that my quest is over and I've found my answers. But I found more than that, Missy. I found you."

"I. . ." She was speechless.

"And I don't ever want to let you go." His final words were a breath upon her mouth as he lowered his head and kissed her, making her heart drop then soar with stunned delight.

The gentle brush of his warm lips against hers grew stronger, and she lifted her arms to wrap them around his neck. She pressed in closer, but he edged away.

"We should go. This would be a splendid time to take a walk in the fresh air."

Giddy from the warmth of his kisses, she giggled and nodded, hardly daring to believe her dreams were really coming true.

Always before, something had come along to pop her fantasy balloon of the life she yearned for; always she'd lost her idyllic dream before it even began. First, with her mother's stinging rejection of her as the child she'd been. Later, with a gangster's unwelcome desire for her as the woman she'd become. Her life had never been happy or normal, even though that had been her dream and all she'd ever wanted.

She would not lose her dream with Peter.

fourteen

As the days slipped into weeks, Peter and Missy's love for each other flourished, while his concern for her sharpened. Neither Guido nor his associates had made an appearance at the restaurant for some time, and while that should produce relief and alleviate his worries, it did the opposite. He couldn't help but recall the words of his mystery host at the soup kitchen: *Don't second-guess Guido and his bunch. For all their foolishness, they are smart and will act when you least expect them to.*

"Peter?"

Missy's voice broke into his thoughts, and he looked up from Mr. Harper's journal he'd opened, though he hadn't been able to concentrate on it. With a mischievous smile, she moved toward him in the empty restaurant and sank to his lap, her mood playful as she plucked off his hat and tossed it to the table.

"Why are you being such a Gloomy Gus today, hm?" She kissed him lightly on the lips. "Ever since you arrived, you've been brooding. It's so unlike you, Peter."

He looked into her beautiful blue eyes, shining with the same love he felt for her. "Missy, will you be my wife?"

"Of course."

"And you will come back with me to England?"

"Tu casa es mi casa." She cradled his jaw with her hands and kissed him again.

He pulled back. "I'm serious, Missy. I wish to marry you. Today."

Her eyes widened. "Peter, I. . .don't know what to say."

These past weeks, they'd spoken of the future when they might one day marry, but their light talk had been in fun, sharing in the fantasy. He'd never formally proposed to her. These strong feelings for Missy he'd experienced since coming to America were a first for him, too, and now he followed the urgings of his heart. Placing his hands at either side of her waist, he lifted her to stand, then dropped to one knee before her. He took her hand in both of his and looked up at her.

Shocked wonderment crossed her features, but the anticipation in her eyes encouraged him to continue.

"Melissa Reynolds, without you I am half a man, and I want to be whole again. You've taken my heart; it is yours. Now I ask you to take all of me. Say we can we be together for a lifetime, whole in each other, our hearts beating as one." He pressed his lips against her hand, closing his eyes, the depth of his emotion threatening to overwhelm him. "With you by my side, I will have found my greatest treasure."

She dropped to her knees before him. "Oh, Peter—yes!" Her hands went to either side of his face, and she drew his head down to kiss him. "Yes, I'll marry you, yes, yes. . ." She kissed him twice more then drew away. "Only. . ."

"Only?" His elation at her response began to fade.

"I can't marry you today. The state has laws. We'll have to wait—I've heard it takes days to get a license." Her eyes sparkled. "Next week is Thanksgiving. The day after Thanksgiving, I'll marry you."

He leaned in close to kiss her again, this sharing of their hearts slow and tender. A smattering of giggles broke them apart, and they looked up to see Rosa enter the room, followed by a clearly agitated Maria. Her dark brows arched high. Both Missy and Peter hurried awkwardly to their feet.

"There is an explanation for this, *sì?*" Maria waved her arm toward the front of the restaurant. "Perhaps you wish to give our customer a sideshow?"

Missy inhaled a sharp breath, her face going pink, and Peter felt just as awkward to realize that an elderly man had slipped into the restaurant, his smile wide as he looked their way.

"I'm not one bit offended, Maria," the man said. "I rather enjoy watching a good proposal."

"Proposal?" Maria swung her gaze to Missy.

"Yes, Maria." Missy's smile brightened her entire face, though her manner seemed nervous. "Peter and I are getting married!"

"Ah, *mi niña!*" Maria strongly embraced Missy, then did the same to Peter. She surveyed them both, an arm around each of their waists. "You do not know how happy this makes me. I have waited long for this day."

"Really, Maria?" Missy's expression seemed doubtful.

"*Sí.* Really, Missy."

Relief flitted across Missy's features. Maria smiled, then clapped her hands together. "I will make a special meal! Daniel, today your dinner will be on the house."

"Well, now," the newcomer said. "It seems as if my timing was perfect after all."

They all laughed, and Peter watched Missy, admiring her beauty and spirit. Still, his niggling worry persisted.

Next week, she would be safe, and he comforted himself with that thought. After their wedding, he would take her with him to Ithaca, New York, where he would embark on his final undertaking. They would remain until late spring or early summer, once any threats of ice on the ocean melted. Then they would sail home to England.

Only a week longer, and she would be safe.

☙

Thanksgiving Day on Thirty-fourth Street was a sight to behold. Crowds of thousands lined the streets in anticipation of the big parade. Children squealed and squirmed, eager for their first view of the floats. Parents hushed and held on to the smallest of their youngsters, while the older ones banded together in groups, pushing toward the front, hoping to get a good place in line.

From 145th Street and Convent Avenue, to 110th Street and Eighth Avenue, on to Thirty-fourth Street and Broadway, the promised three-hour parade brought New Yorkers out by the masses. Exhilaration zipped through the icy air, and though snow lightly frosted the heads of the waiting crowd, it couldn't dampen their excitement.

Melissa stood with Peter, her gloved hand encased in his as they waited with the rest of the crowd and craned their heads at the first faint strains of band music—trumpets, horns, and drums.

"It's coming," a young boy cried out. "The parade is coming!"

The people cheered and waved pennants, their arms, and their hands. Caught up in the excitement, Melissa and Peter did the same. Her smile was bright for another reason; beneath her glove, a diamond engagement ring circled her finger. Peter had told her four days ago when they went to pick it out that even though their engagement would be short, he wanted her to have it all. She had stared at him in some amazement.

"But if you're not an heir to the title, can we afford such an extravagance?"

He had laughed and kissed her cheek, mentioning that his father, Lawrence, had put aside a yearly allowance for him. "But I love to paint, and my dabblings have fetched a good price among those lords and ladies interested."

"You paint? What do you paint?"

"Landscapes, though I've done a few portraits; I'm told I'm quite good, actually."

"I believe it. You would succeed in anything you put your mind to, Peter."

"You think so? I'd like to paint you one day. You inspire me. In fact, I wish I had a canvas with me this very moment."

She had giggled. "Yes, I can just see you setting up camp on the sidewalk right here in front of Macy's, with your easel and your paints."

Now as she stood beside him, viewing the parade, her dreams sailed through her heart on ribbons of promise, much like the massive helium balloons that billowed and floated past the skyscrapers. She looked to the sky to see the first one approach.

Marchers carried ropes that secured the balloons and kept them from flying away before it was time. This was the second year Macy's had used them. Last year, the balloons burst once they were released, and she hoped the man in charge had fixed the problem and it wouldn't happen again. It had been rather disconcerting to see Felix the Cat blown to smithereens.

Melissa pointed out to Peter the mammoth colorful toy-soldier balloon floating above a few live camels and elephants guided by their trainers. She thought she heard her name and looked over her shoulder. To her surprise, she glimpsed Rosa's face and red hood about twenty feet away. The young girl looked around, as though searching for someone, and Melissa tugged Peter's sleeve, motioning to her cousin. "We should go to her," she yelled above the cheering crowd and blaring music. Still he couldn't hear and shook his head, leaning in closer. She cupped her hand around his ear. "Rosa is over there. We should go to her. She looks lost."

He straightened and nodded, his gaze going to where she pointed. Hand in hand, they slowly made their way through the press of bodies. Many parade-goers acted disgruntled or mouthed irate comments that Melissa was glad she couldn't hear. She tried to keep a good grip on Peter's hand, but people pushed between them. She felt the pull of her arm as she attempted to hold on and then the sudden loss of his touch.

"Peter?" She tried to turn around, but a heavyset man terminated her efforts as he shoved into her. People moved closer to see the next float. "Peter!"

Abandoning her efforts and hoping he hadn't lost sight of her and could catch up, she focused ahead.

"Rosa!" she called, the name a bare scrape of sound amid the sudden clamor of numerous cymbals crashing. Her cousin showed no sign of having heard her.

Someone grabbed Melissa's arm. "Hey!"

Another strong hand grabbed her other arm. "Don't make a sound, and we'll let your boyfriend live. Understand?" a male voice rasped in her ear.

Fear knotted her throat, but she gave an abrupt nod.

"Good girl. Now, walk with us real nice-like and no funny business. You try anything, and my friend Bernardo here will introduce your British boyfriend to the darker side of Manhattan. Got it?"

She swallowed hard. In the close press of bodies, she felt the outline of a revolver in the man's shoulder holster. Again she nodded.

"You're one real smart doll. Come on. The boss wants to see you." Gruffly, he and his friend forced Melissa to walk with them toward the back of the crowd.

Through the fear swirling round her mind, one thought broke through and soared upward in a silent plea. *Please God, don't let anything happen to Peter.*

❧

The moment Missy's hand slipped from his, a thread of worry wound around Peter's mind. He struggled through the crowd. Because of his limp, his endeavors proved difficult, especially with those who made no move to let him pass and grew belligerent when he shoved through anyway, as if by moving aside and allowing him to obstruct their view for mere seconds they would miss the entire parade.

Worry thickened into dread when Peter could find no sign of Missy. In desperation, he scanned the faces of those around him but spotted no green velvet hat or brown coat. He managed to quicken his pace and came up beside Rosa.

"Where's Missy?" he asked in greeting.

Her expression of pleasure to see him faded into anxiety. "Melissa? I thought she was with you."

"We became separated." Again, he searched the area, scanning faces and forms. The tail end of one of the marching bands passed, and hearing became easier. "Where are your parents?"

"Papa wasn't feeling well, and Mama wanted to stay and work on preparations for the wedding."

The wedding. Peter swallowed down the metallic taste of fear and fought to keep it from spiraling out of control. He took hold of her upper arm in a tight grip so as not to lose her. "Come, you must help me find her. We'll stay together, but you look in that direction, I'll look in this one."

She nodded and walked with him as Peter retraced his steps. He stumbled, almost tripping over something. Rosa bent to pick up the object. As she straightened, alarm threatened to consume him when he saw what she held.

"Melissa's purse." Her brown eyes were very wide and scared.

Any hope that foul play wasn't involved quickly dissolved into despair. "Rosa, can you find your way back home on your own?"

"*Sí.* I came alone."

"I want you to go home. Now."

"But the parade, it is not over. And Melissa, she is lost."

"Just do as I say." He softened his brusque words with a faded smile of encouragement. "Please. You must tell your parents what happened. They need to notify the police."

Her eyes widened even more. "I will go now."

Peter watched her thread her way to the buildings at the back; then he turned to ask several people if they'd seen Missy, giving a brief description of her. The few who cooperated in giving him an answer said they hadn't been paying any attention to those around them, only to the parade.

Dear God, how will I find her?

He worked his way to the back where another street intersected. Glad to see it reasonably empty, he hurried as fast as he was able, hoping to find a taxicab. Frantic, he had no idea how to begin his search—or where. He sucked in a deep breath, forcing himself to think.

First he would return to the restaurant, speak with Tony, and find out where Guido lived. Wherever that man hid, Peter felt certain he would find Missy there.

&

The thugs on either side of Melissa forced her to walk between the buildings and down an empty street, then bundled her into the back of a waiting Lincoln. She quickly slid over the seat, but before she could get a grip on the opposite door handle, one of Guido's men jumped in beside her and grabbed her arm.

"Any more of that and we'll have to tie you up. Behave!"

She detested being spoken to like a child, especially from this ruffian who could hardly be described as acting mature. "Where are you taking me?"

He leered. "The boss wants to see you, and I aim to follow orders. And lady, if that means I have to knock you out cold to get you there, then that's what I'll do."

Melissa sank back, crossing her arms over her chest out of cold, fear, and anger.

"That's better." He nodded to the man in front, who turned to the steering wheel. The car took off like a shot, throwing Melissa's head back against the seat. Her guard, a husky Italian with a wide forehead and eyes that were dark both in color and intent, pulled a silver flask from his pocket and unscrewed it, taking a large swig. He pulled it away from his mouth, offering the bootleg liquor to Melissa, but she wrinkled her nose in disgust and turned her head away.

He laughed and made a snide comment. Melissa chose not to rise to the bait. At some point, she might be able to escape from these men. Until then, she dared not annoy them at the risk of having her hands and feet tied.

The thought that her wedding day was tomorrow struck her, and she squeezed her eyes shut, refusing to let these bullies see her reduced to tears.

Dear God, please open a way of escape.

fifteen

"I told you, I don't know." His hands cupping his head, Peter threaded his fingers through his hair in frustration. "She was directly in front of me."

The police inspector asking questions chewed on the end of his cigar and pinpointed Peter with shrewd eyes. "So you're saying you didn't see anyone nab her?"

"No, I didn't."

"Well, now, in a crowd of thousands, it doesn't seem so unusual that you two got separated. Happens all the time. She's probably out there right now, walking around Macy's and trying to find you."

Grabbing Missy's purse, Peter rose from his chair and approached the man, who seemed intent on finding excuses for why he shouldn't start a search. He held it up. "I found this on the ground. It's her handbag. Now I don't know if you understand anything about women, Inspector, but a woman would not simply drop her handbag and leave it lying on the ground for it to be trodden upon."

"In the press of the crowd, she might not have realized she dropped it until it was too late."

"That is highly unlikely."

The man took a puff from his cigar.

"Why aren't you out there looking for her?" Peter tried to cage his frustration, but with every minute that passed with Missy unaccounted for, irritation was fast breaking through the iron bars of his reserve. "Instead of asking me these ridiculous questions, you should be out trying to catch the criminal who abducted her. I'll even give you a name—Guido Piccoli. Once you find him, I'm certain you'll find Missy."

Peter sensed Tony stiffen beside him. A cold look crusted the inspector's eyes. "You have proof he took her, evidence of some kind?"

"No." Peter felt any credence his words might have received dissipate like smoke. "Just a hunch."

"A hunch, he says." He glanced at the uniformed officer beside him, and both men had the audacity to smile. "Mr. Caldwell, we can't just go around arresting people without grounds to do so. It's like I said, she probably got lost and will be walking through that door any minute."

"I can't believe this." Peter began to pace, then faced them. "So you're not going to do anything?"

"We can't very well act unless we establish that a crime has been committed. If she hasn't returned by morning, give us a call." He tipped his hat to Maria, who stood pale and trembling in the circle of Tony's arms. Rosa sat in a chair by Maria, her downcast gaze focused on the floor.

All manner of words soared to Peter's lips as the policemen made their exits, but he dared not utter a one of them.

"You should not have mentioned Guido," Tony said. "I have no proof, but I think for many months some on the police force are owned by Vittorio. His family rules many in New York. If this is so, and these policemen take orders from him, they will not work hard to find her."

Then whom could a person trust? Peter wanted to ask but didn't when he observed the pained horror in Maria's eyes.

"Tomorrow was your wedding day," she said sadly, taking his hand in both of hers.

"I'll find her." Peter tried to reach through her fear and make her believe. "I promise."

"How?" Tony asked. "Where will you go?"

"Do you know where Guido lives?"

"No, I don't. I'm sorry."

Peter nodded and picked up his hat, setting it on his head. "Then I must go see someone who does." His gaze again went to Maria. "I *will* find her."

❧

The Packard stopped in front of a ritzy establishment that Melissa assumed lay on the outskirts of Manhattan. The glow of incandescent light flooded the windows of both stories beyond the closed draperies. They'd taken back streets, often rough with ruts, and Melissa had lost track of their course. She wondered if the roundabout route was intentional, if Guido had warned his men about her excellent sense of direction and aptitude for finding locales. He would know anything about her that Uncle Tony might have chosen to share over the years.

Pity for her uncle seeped into her heart. She didn't blame Tony for his respectful fear of the nephew of the infamous Vittorio; every man who knew the family or knew of them dreaded what they could do. All except Peter. If he feared them, he hadn't shown it. Still, her aunt had taught her that even the bravest of men possessed a measure of fear but had learned the secret of how to conquer it by not allowing it to inhabit them.

Melissa prayed for that same courage.

One of her two abductors knocked on the door in a signal. Almost immediately, a flapper opened it, the shoulders of her red-fringed dress askew, her eyes half closed and bleary from too much whiskey, if her breath was anything to go by. She gave Melissa a cursory glance, then let out a laughing snort.

"You know where to take her, boys."

They walked farther into the mansion, and Melissa caught sight of a parlor before they went through a door and into an empty room, a man's study, by the look of the brown and gold furnishings and the massive desk off in a corner. One of the men moved to the paneled wall, reaching behind the fireplace mantel.

The entire wall moved outward as if on a hinge, and Melissa gaped. Both men forced her into a dark corridor beyond; the wall closed behind them. A cord was pulled, and a light bulb flickered on, weakly shining down on them. On both sides of the corridor, tall racks held wine bottles. They continued along the hidden passageway to a crude wooden door. From beyond it, Melissa heard loud jazz music, laughing, and talking.

One of the men knocked, again using a signal. A wooden slat in the door shot to the side, revealing a square opening and a pair of eyes. Melissa took an involuntary step back. The ogre who held her left arm tightened his grip as if afraid she might run. *Run?* she thought wryly. *Where?* Even if she could get back to the mock-fireplace door, she had no idea how to open it.

The wooden slat shot back into place, the sound of a heavy bolt scraped across the door, and it opened wide.

Melissa coughed, and her eyes watered at the rank smell of cigarette smoke. The entire room, lavish with its red and gold furnishings, lay smothered in a cloud of smoke that made it seem cheap. Women, most of them flappers judging by their brash clothes and attitudes, sat with men, danced with them, drank with them. Uniformed waiters glided past several small tables and chairs, carrying trays of drinks. Couples in embrace occupied two sofas, and a group of men gambled with a roulette wheel in a far corner. The place lay smothered in a pit of darkness; the lamps and the lights of the chandelier turned down low.

Spared from having to associate with the speakeasy's inhabitants, Melissa was hurried along as her jailers escorted her to the back of the huge room and to another door. She ignored the curious glances many flappers turned toward her, as well as the interested stares their male companions gave.

One of her abductors used the same knock. The door swung open, and a tall man, at least two heads taller than Melissa, glared at them. His gaze dropped to Melissa, and he motioned them inside with a quick jerk of his head.

She walked into another plush room and abruptly halted.

In a chair in front of the fireplace, Guido sat with lazy

elegance. His gaze slowly swept over her, and then he smiled, like a sleek panther that had triumphed over its prey.

❧

Peter found the soup kitchen with little trouble. His former host proved more difficult to locate. Men and women crowded the area, but Peter soon spotted the man's familiar tall form and hurried his way.

"Hello," the Frenchman said with a smile. "I did not expect to see you here again."

"I need your help," Peter greeted. "Guido and his men have taken my fiancée, and I need you to help me locate them."

A grave look swept into his host's eyes, and he cast a glance around as if afraid of being overheard. "We can't talk here. Come outside."

Peter walked with him to the door. The moment the salty tang of ocean air hit his face, Peter turned to him. "I need you to tell me where Guido's home is located."

"Why do you think I would know?" Wariness touched the words.

"You told me you were one of them once; did you know Guido, too?"

"It was a long time ago, and I worked for Vittorio, not Guido. But if you think you can just march into their home and take your fiancée back, you are sadly mistaken, *mon ami.*"

Peter pulled his coat to the side to reveal Tony's concealed gun. The Frenchman only raised his brows and laughed. "You seriously think you can do damage with that relic? These men have machine guns and all the latest in handguns—many of them."

"I have to find her and bring her back. I won't rest until I do."

He surveyed Peter a long moment. "There is a speakeasy ten miles from here. A wealthy widow's home. If Guido wanted to hide someone, I think he would choose that place. He spends much time there, I am told." He went on to give detailed directions, and Peter felt thankful he'd spent so much time searching through Manhattan and recognized many of the street names. Yet one matter disturbed him.

"I thought you didn't know Guido."

"*Non.* I never said that. He was only a young man when I quit working for the family, still much of a boy."

For the first time, Peter wondered if he could really trust this man; Tony had told him that the underworld had spies everywhere.

As if reading his mind, the Frenchman straightened. "I am not giving you false information, nor would I become the informer and rat on you. As God is my witness, I have no evil intent. You already know what danger you face."

"Why did you quit working for the family?"

"I had become the next name on the list."

"The list?"

"They intended to kill me; an associate warned me, and I escaped."

Peter's eyes narrowed. "And you're not afraid they'll find you now?"

He chuckled dryly. "They would never think to look for me in this place." He waved his hand toward the mission. "Years have passed; they have forgotten one insignificant Frenchman."

From what Tony had told him, Peter doubted Guido or his family would forget anything. He stared at the man before him a moment longer before nodding, satisfied. "Thank you for your help." He turned to go.

"You are really going to do this alone?"

"I have no choice."

His host gave a swift nod and stuck out his hand. Peter took it, and both men clasped forearms.

"Then I will pray for you, *mon ami.* For in order to succeed, you will surely need guidance as you have never needed it before."

sixteen

Melissa remained quiet, though every nerve ending stood on alert. Guido sat in casual elegance, his Italian good looks belying the hard glint in his eyes that spoke of his ruthlessness. With unhurried grace, he poured amber liquid into a crystal glass. He rose and approached, holding the glass out to her.

"You look parched, my dear Melissa. Have a drink to quench your thirst."

Giving no thought to her actions, she knocked the glass from his hand with one sweep. It went crashing to the floor, and liquid splashed up onto the wall.

"No, thank you," she said with ultra politeness, though her tone oozed a chill that frosted the room. "I'm not interested in anything you have to offer."

His eyes narrowed; his jaw hardened. After tense seconds, he gave the slightest nod as if he'd figured her out and smiled, though there was no warmth to his expression. He looked past Melissa. With an abrupt jerk of his head, he motioned for his lackeys to leave the room. Melissa swallowed, made uneasier now that the two of them were alone.

"That's one quality I've always admired about you, Melissa. You have such fire and spirit encased in that cool, blond veneer."

To escape his close proximity, she sought the warmth of the fire. Pulling off a glove so as to warm her hands, she tried to appear unruffled, but her pulse beat rapidly in her throat, giving her fear away. One thing stood in her favor; Guido seemed to admire women of courage, and she had no intention of falling to her knees and begging for him to release her like some melodramatic heroine from a silent movie. If she kept her wits about her, by some miracle she might persuade him to see reason and return her to her family.

"Maybe you'd care to tell me why your thugs spirited me away from an absolutely delightful parade, only to bring me to this dark, dreary place." Careful to keep her tone civil, she arched her eyebrows in question and pulled off the other glove. As she did, she realized her mistake. Guido's eyes clouded as dark as a thunderstorm at the flash of her ring. He rushed her way and grabbed her by the shoulders.

"He'll never have you, Melissa—you're mine! I've waited for you to grow up for a long time."

Disconcerted, fear clotted her throat, and she held the flaps of her coat together. "I never belonged to you; I don't want to belong to you. My pastor teaches that light can't live with darkness. Neither will survive that kind of union. We serve two different masters, Guido. I serve the Almighty God; you serve the god of mammon."

His chuckle was dark. "What? So pious all of a sudden?"

"Which proves you know nothing about me. I respect God, even if I don't always understand His methods. I could never live this kind of life."

His hands dropped from her shoulders. "Ah, but Melissa, I would give you everything you could ever want. Fur coats, a house of your own, a car with your own chauffeur. . ." He sauntered behind her, reaching around to trace her jaw with his knuckle. Her mouth dry with alarm, she jerked her head away from his touch. He moved his finger lower to glide across her neck. "Diamonds, pearls, rubies. . .whatever your heart desires to decorate that white throat—it's yours."

"I'm not interested in the accumulation of such goods if I have to sell my soul to gain them."

He came around to face her again, his expression amused. "So you think I am the devil?"

"I think you act like the devil. You could do so much good with all your money and power, but instead you choose to cause others only pain and harm."

He lost his seductive quality and straightened, almost defensive. His black eyes glittered. "I give the people what they want."

"That's just a poor excuse to feed their bad habits and to supply yourself with even more money in the process. And you know it."

He laughed. "You really are such a child. It is time you grew up and opened your eyes to the reality of the world. It's not some fairytale land of your daydreams. It's harsh, it's cruel, and if people choose to indulge in a few harmless pleasures to lighten their loads, then what harm is there in that?"

His words brought to mind her own cherished dream, and she furrowed her brow as once again she realized her fantasy balloon had been blown to smithereens. There would be no wedding for her tomorrow.

"You will change your mind," he said with confidence. "Spend a night or two locked inside this room without food or water, and you may find the prospect of my company isn't so disagreeable."

"Never."

Her emphatic declaration only made him laugh. "We shall see, Melissa. We shall see."

She was fast growing to despise that name.

❧

Peter sat in the back of the taxicab, wishing to increase the vehicle's speed, though the cabbie drove as fast as the car could manage down several dark, rutted streets and past buildings of questionable repute.

Looking out the side window, Peter grew alert. "Stop!"

The driver hit the brakes with a screech, then looked back at Peter with a doubtful expression on his craggy face. "You want to get out here?"

"I see someone I need to talk with."

"Okay, fellah. That'll be a buck-eighty."

"I'll be coming back directly."

The cabbie shook his head. "I ain't stickin' around these parts; you want me to drop you somewhere else, I will. You want out now, the fare's up. I've been robbed in this area before, and I ain't temptin' fate again."

"Very well." Peter firmed his jaw and paid the man, then approached the woman who'd just exited one of the ramshackle buildings that looked as if it should be condemned.

"Well, well. If it isn't the English prince come to visit us common peasants," Florence said in greeting. "Did ya lose your proper lady, or are you out looking for some real fun?"

Peter ignored her snide words. "I need you to help me get into the speakeasy that Guido runs."

Her eyes widened. "Oh, no. Nothin' doin'." She gave an incredulous laugh. "You realize his men know what you look like? You wouldn't be able to get within a hundred yards of that place and not be spotted. And I've got a newsflash for you, Mr. Royal Bucks—Guido doesn't like you."

"I mean to do my best to find a way inside. He's abducted Missy."

"Is that a fact? Well, I'm sorry, but I'm not getting involved."

"If you'll help me," he said before she took more than three steps away from him, "we'll both get what we want."

She turned, her eyes sparking with curious interest. "Oh, how's that?"

"You'll have Guido, and I'll have Missy."

Taken aback, she reeled before making a quick recovery, but he didn't deny that she cared for the mobster, though Peter couldn't begin to fathom why.

"If you're caught, it's curtains for you. And you know what that means?" she asked.

Peter nodded. "No matter; I have to do this."

In disbelief, she stared at him, as if just coming to a realization. "You really love her."

"She's my life," he said simply.

A wistful flicker touched her eyes but quickly vanished.

Clearly agitated, she looked at him, looked away, and shook her head. "I can't believe I'm doing this," she muttered under her breath, then said to him, "I can get you through the door, but after that, you're on your own. If you're caught, I had nothing to do with any of it."

"Agreed."

"Oh, all right then." She shook her head, giving him a weak smile. "So tell me, are all British gentlemen knights in armor in disguise?"

She found them another cab. Fifteen minutes later, the driver pulled up to the drive of a two-story mansion.

After Peter paid the man and the cab took off, Florence eyed Peter in appraisal, as if she found him wanting. "First thing we need to do is make you look like you've had a night out on the town." She studied his clothes, frowning, and popped off his hat. With one hand she mussed his hair so that it hung over his forehead, then slapped his hat back on his head. Her brow wrinkled in displeasure. "Button up your coat. . .no, mismatch the buttons to the holes. Make it hang crooked. Hmm. . ."

Peter stood silent, allowing her to continue her ministrations. She tugged his collar high up around his neck, then lowered her assessing gaze to his cane. "Can you lose that? It's a dead giveaway."

"I'll need the support. I may stumble otherwise."

"That's the whole idea, Romeo, just until we get through the door and mix with the crowd. You can lean on me—that'll give your disguise even more of a convincing effect. Gretta expects that of the men I bring to her establishment."

"Her establishment?"

"Guido uses Gretta's home for a cover. Look, do you wanna do this or not?"

"Most definitely." All Peter could think about was the danger Missy was in.

They walked to the door, keeping to the shadows. At Florence's order, Peter hooked his cane in his waistband and again buttoned his coat. Florence anchored her arm around Peter's waist, supporting him. "Lean on my neck," she whispered. "And lower that hat. If she sees those clear blue eyes of yours, she'll know right off the bat she's being hoodwinked. Your face is too angelic looking as it is, but your eyes give away the fact you haven't been drinking."

A dark-haired woman dressed in flapper style, much like Florence, opened the door to a signal knock.

"He looks like he's had too much already," Gretta said after the two women exchanged greetings.

Peter hoped he wasn't overacting the part required of him. He sensed the woman's mistrust and lowered his head.

"Now, Gretta," Florence said with a carefree laugh. "When is it *ever* too much?"

That got the woman laughing, and she opened the door wider to let them inside. Soon Peter found himself in a large den, and Florence quickly shut the door behind them. "One more hurdle, and you're through," she said in an undertone as she tripped a hidden lever and the fireplace wall opened.

"My word." Stunned, he stared at the dark corridor beyond and shook his head.

"Come on, Sir Knight," Florence urged, putting her arm around him and supporting him as he walked beside her.

Another bolted door barred their entrance at the end of the long corridor. A secret knock and a brief appraisal by the hulking man inside the door, and Peter entered what appeared to be a den of iniquity. Jazz music zinged through the crimson and gold room from a player piano. Women in skimpy fringed dresses showed the tops of their stockings as they kicked their heels high to do the Charleston. For a moment, Peter hesitated; he'd never been inside such a place and felt ill that Guido had brought Missy here. What manner of evil had he subjected her to? Peter clenched his teeth, fighting down a surge of anger.

"I'll just leave you over there by the wall—there's a door at the back that leads to a private parlor. I have a feeling if she's anywhere, he would've put her in there. I don't see her out here."

They staggered through the room, and Peter leaned heavily against Florence until they reached the wall. No one paid them any attention, since several others stumbled about the room in the same condition. "This is where I leave you off, Romeo. From this point on, I'm out of the picture."

"Thank you." He hoped his eyes conveyed the depth of his gratitude. "You're a very kind woman, Florence."

"Yeah, sure." She gave a wry snort, but her expression lost a bit of its hard edge. "Just don't let the word get around, or it'll ruin my reputation. Good luck."

It would take much more than luck. Only God's intervention could help him in this situation, and Peter knew it. He hadn't planned beyond this moment and had no idea how he would get Missy out of this place. He certainly couldn't bring her through this room full of people or past the gun-toting guards posted near the doors. With relief, he saw the door at the back was unguarded.

At the fringes of the dim room, Peter unbuttoned his coat and carefully removed his cane. One thing stood in his favor: with all the revelry and loud music, he would be surprised if anyone noticed him.

He moved to the door and tried the handle. It wouldn't budge.

seventeen

Missy stood by the fireplace where Guido had left her and surveyed the furnishings of her gilded prison. A small chandelier glittered from the ceiling. Decorated in red and gold like the room next door, this parlor reminded her of a room a Greek palace might contain. A massive gold-framed painting of women in Grecian dress hung on one rose-papered wall, and a plush matching sofa stood angled in the center. Little else filled the room. No windows lined the walls for her to slip out of; no other doors lay in wait for her exit.

She shivered, drawing her coat tighter around her, and rubbed her arms. The fire in the grate couldn't dispel the chill closing in around her heart. He would be back, whether tonight or tomorrow, and she sensed the next time he wouldn't be so tolerant of her refusal. Guido always took what he wanted, but when he returned, she would be ready for him.

She scanned the room for a weapon and noticed a heavy brass candlestick on one of the side tables that flanked the sofa. If Guido came back tonight to carry out his intent, she would show him she wasn't some docile lamb to be naively led to the slaughter. Now that she stood alone in the locked room and the shock of her abduction had faded, fear also had lost its razor edge.

The candlestick base was slim enough to slip the article inside her deep coat pocket and heavy enough to knock any-one out. She pulled the tapered candle from its holder and slid the candlestick inside her coat. Confident that she at least had that to use in defense, she wandered to the sofa and sank onto it.

No magazines or books sat on either of the two tables, and Missy sought about for something to pass the time. Thoughts of Peter and her terminated wedding day weakened her and brought tears, so she forced her mind to other things. She had to stay emotionally alert and strong; she couldn't afford to break down now, not until this was over. And it *would* be over.

She recalled other memories, ones that helped firm her resolve and kept a sharp point on her indignation. Her mind touched upon the memory of her mother abandoning her to run off with her fourth husband, and for the briefest moment, Missy wondered where her mother was, if she was well, and if a number five had been added to her list of conquests. Her mother's desire for men's attention almost made Missy pity her. She recalled that last night on the *Titanic*, and how, when she had left her bed to ask for a drink, she had caught the cabin steward in her mother's arms. Painful as was the memory of her mother's stinging slap delivered after taking Missy back to bed, it did not hurt like the words hissed in her face, claiming Missy was always in the way.

As the minutes passed, though Missy had no clock to show her just how many, apathy once more gave way to apprehension, and she turned to prayer again.

"Father, I am so frightened, but I know somehow You will protect me from Guido. Keep my family and Peter safe, and please help me find a way out of this place." She gave a cursory glance to the four rose-colored walls surrounding her. "There must be a way. . . ."

Thinking of the false fireplace, she moved toward the mantel. If the other room hid a passage, this room might, too. She ran her hands over the carved marble, but her fingers didn't make contact with a hidden lever or knob. Not ready to admit defeat, she tried again, more slowly this time, sliding her fingertips over every inch of the smooth surface, pressing any recesses she found. Biting her lower lip in contemplation, she turned to look at the rest of the room. Her attention went to the door. To her alarm, she noticed the knob turning.

She dipped her hand into her pocket and withdrew the

candlestick. Hiding it behind her back, she watched as the door swung slowly open.

❧

Peter used the key Florence had given him. Earlier, he'd spotted her across the room and made eye contact, signaling the door was locked. In tense amazement, he'd watched as she nodded and moved toward a tall man in a black, pinstriped suit and fedora, who looked like one of the mobsters. She flirted with him while pulling his coat lapels together and drew him out to dance with her. A few minutes later, she walked past Peter, slipping the key into his pocket. Peter assumed she must have used sleight of hand to retrieve it, because he'd watched the entire time and the man never handed the key to Florence.

A commotion at the front brought Peter's head around in worry that he'd been caught. A strange pair walked into the speakeasy—an ugly woman in a knee-length, brown fur coat and a man with a black beard down to his chest. Something about them and their loud demand for two gin and tonics seemed unusual, but he didn't stop to consider. Quickly, he slipped into the room, praying Missy would be there, and closed the door behind him. Even over the jazz music, he heard the sound of metal striking stone and swung his gaze to the right.

Missy stared at him, her eyes wide, a candlestick rolling near her feet.

She rushed toward him at the same time he went to her. Her hands grabbed either side of his head, and he reached for her as she peppered fervent kisses across his mouth and jaw. His relief at finding her safe made his own response just as intense, and he kissed her over and over again, wondering if the tears he felt against his cheek were hers or his own.

"Are you both completely loco?" Florence asked, having followed him in and closed the door. "Someone could walk into this room any second, so if you two lovebirds can stop your pecking now, we really should get you out of here."

Missy turned in shock, moving her hands to circle Peter's arm.

"Florence? What are you doing here?"

"Believe me, I've asked myself that question for the past half hour, ever since your lover boy roped me into doing this." She looked at the closed door as if afraid it would suddenly swing open. "We don't have a lot of time. I think someone spotted me slipping the key out of Bernardo's pocket. I don't know if they'd rat on me or not, but I don't want to take any chances."

Peter slipped his arm protectively around Missy. "Can you get her a disguise, a scarf or something of that nature? Her blond hair is sure to draw attention, as light as it is."

"Oh, you can't go back out there. That would be suicide."

"Then how?" Missy sounded confused. "There's no other way out."

"Honey," Florence said with a dry chuckle, "there's always a way out if you look hard enough."

Florence walked toward the fireplace just as the door banged open. One of Guido's men burst inside. Peter pushed Missy down to safety behind the sofa and pulled out Tony's gun before the guard could reach for his. He'd never shot a man and didn't think he could now. Instead, he aimed for the chandelier chain and fired. The crystal light crashed down on the hoodlum's head, and he sank, unconscious, to the floor.

Florence raced to shut the door and wedged the sole chair in the room beneath the knob. "You've both got to get out of here, now!" Even as she spoke, the door shook on its hinges with the force of the blows aimed against it. "This chair won't keep them out long."

"But how do we get out?" Missy looked at the walls as though she expected a door to materialize before them.

"The left andiron—twist it to the right. And hurry!" Florence added when the wooden door almost shattered.

Missy sped to the fireplace and twisted the gold andiron. A click sounded, barely discernable over the banging against the door. She looked around the room to locate the source, then toward Florence, her face a mask of confusion.

"The painting—push on it. The passage'll take you to a room on the other side of the house that leads to a door outside. But you have to hurry. They know about the passage—it was created in case of a raid."

Peter pushed on the painting, and it swung inward. He stepped over a two-foot high ledge that was part of the wall and turned to help Missy, just as the door crashed inward, the chair flew aside, and Florence screamed.

eighteen

Shocked, Missy looked back. Bernardo caught her eye and raced for the opening, grabbing her arm before she could escape.

"Oh, no you don't!" He yanked on her arm so hard he almost pulled her off her feet. Missy acted before she thought. Wrenching back her other arm, she swung with all she had in her, and her fist connected with his eye. He let go and staggered backward, cupping his hand over it. Before he could lurch at Missy again, Florence hit him over the head with the crystal decanter, and he sank to the floor.

Peter stared at Missy, his mouth agape.

She shrugged self-consciously and shook her stinging hand. "I did mention my uncle once gave me boxing lessons."

Despite the gravity of the situation, Peter grinned, then turned his attention to Florence. "Come on!" he urged, holding out his hand.

"Oh, no." She shook her head. "But you two had better skedaddle before Guido and his big ape get back. These two bozos were easy enough to tangle with, but the others are much more dangerous."

High-pitched whistles suddenly pierced the air, and ladies screeched from the next room. Florence's jaw dropped.

"What is it?" Missy asked.

"A raid! The feds have found the place."

"Then you haven't got a choice now!" Peter grabbed Florence's arm and hauled her inside the passageway. He closed the door hidden behind the painting, leaving them in the dark and muting the sounds of pandemonium from the other side.

"Can you lock it?" Peter asked.

"No." Florence's voice shook.

"How will we see?" Missy whispered. "Is there a light somewhere?"

"It's too risky to pull the switch. If someone else comes inside, they'd see us right away. We're just going to have to walk blind and use the wall to feel our way. This passage leads straight to the room with the outside door."

"How do we know the feds haven't surrounded the place?" Missy asked the woman behind her.

"We don't."

Missy didn't like the sound of that. She and Peter were innocent of any nefarious activities associated with the speakeasy, but their presence here argued otherwise. And she didn't want to spend the night in jail on the eve of her wedding.

She closed her eyes, continuing to follow Peter, one hand on his shoulder, the other using the rough rock wall to guide her. In this pitch black, whether she left her eyes opened or closed didn't matter. The popping of gunfire sounded far beyond the painting, and she swallowed hard, praying they wouldn't be found, hoping the federal agents would be successful in their raid.

She forced her spirits to rally; five minutes ago, her prospects had been glum, and she'd entertained the possibility of having to protect her virtue. She hadn't been sure when, if ever, she'd see Peter again, and now she had him with her. Whatever further trial challenged them, at least they were together again.

An eternity seemed to pass before Peter came to an abrupt stop. "We've reached a dead end; I can't go any farther, and I can't find a handle."

"That's the door," Florence said. "Just push hard on it; there is no handle."

Peter did so, and the pitch black lightened to gray as a moonlit room opened before them. They left the passage and closed what looked like part of the paneled wall. When Peter shut it, Missy couldn't see any sign of a door.

"Hurry!" Florence ordered. "But try to be quiet."

They sped across the room to an opposite door, the rapid taps of Peter's cane the only sound on the tiles.

"Can't you keep that thing quieter?" Florence asked in fearful exasperation.

"Sorry." Peter's tone was apologetic.

"Never mind. We'll be outside soon enough, and it won't matter."

Cautiously, she cracked open the last door and peered out. After several seconds she relaxed and pulled it wider. "It's safe."

They moved across the grounds, cutting a path toward some trees at the back of the mansion. From the front, they could hear men and women screaming irate words, and Missy assumed the police were busy hauling the flappers and other drinkers outside to the paddy wagon.

They left the open area and moved toward the shadows of the trees. Suddenly a pair of headlights switched on, spotlighting them. As one, they swung around in shock. An automobile sat concealed within the shadows of trees opposite the road, no more than ten feet away.

&

Peter blinked hard against the glare, drawing Missy close to his side. Florence clutched his other sleeve. The headlights switched off, and the door swung open. A shadowy figure emerged. Peter tensed and reached for Tony's gun, prepared to do battle.

"I figured you could use a getaway car," a man said, his smooth voice breaking the electric silence.

Peter almost laughed in relief. "It's all right," he said to the women as he hurried them toward the car. "He's a friend."

The Frenchman opened the door for them to pile in the back and hurried to resume his place behind the wheel. The car took off at a crawl in the opposite direction from the mansion. Once they were blocks away, he switched on the headlights again and picked up speed. "Where do you wish me to take you?"

"Marelli's Restaurant," Missy said.

"No." Peter looked at her. "It will be the first place Guido looks."

"Your hotel?"

He shook his head. "They know who I am; they could find us there, too."

"Then where?"

"They would never find you at the soup kitchen," their driver said.

"Brilliant!" Peter smiled. "I'll leave the women there and return to the hotel for my things. I'll make a call to your aunt while I'm there, Missy, assuring her you're safe, and then I'll take you to Ithaca."

"Ithaca?" The Frenchman grew alert.

"An acquaintance of my mother's lives there, someone she met on the *Titanic*. They manage a children's reform school, so I believe Missy will be safe in such a secure environment."

Their driver gave no reply, and Peter continued to discuss the details of their plans. Once they arrived at the soup kitchen, their host excused himself to find his wife.

"Well, toodle-oo! I wish you the best." Florence walked away from the car in the opposite direction.

"Wait, don't go," Peter said. She turned to him, her eyes wary, and he continued. "You don't have to go back to Guido and the rest of them."

"I don't, huh? And where else would I go?" She swung her hand to take in the nearby wharf. "Should I take a dive in the ocean?"

Peter's eyes were steady as he walked up to her. "You said something earlier that had great merit. 'There's always a way out if you look hard enough.' It's as I said, Florence, you don't have to go back."

She chuckled wryly at her own words used against her. "You know nothing about me or where I come from, oh privileged prince. I'm not like you; I never had a decent bone in my body. I fought tooth and nail for everything I got, but now it's mine, and I'm happy just as I am." The waver to her biting words proved she wasn't as callous as she tried to make it appear. "Besides, there's no way out for the likes of me. There just isn't."

"There is," Missy said, her expression gentle as she came to stand beside Peter. "The only way out is up."

Before Florence could follow with another retort, a lovely brunette, big with child, approached them. "Hello. You must be Peter. I'm Janine. My husband's told me so much about you." She smiled at Missy and Florence, including them in her greeting. Peter made introductions, and Janine waved her hand toward the soup kitchen door.

"Please, come inside and rest," she said, directing her words to Florence, and Peter wondered how much of their conversation Janine had overheard. "You've all been through so much tonight. My husband will speak soon; you should stay and listen. His words are very powerful."

"Speak?" Peter asked.

"He ministers to those who come here to eat. He tells his story and gives them hope. When we first met, he had just been released from prison and was a hard nut to crack. Believe me!" She laughed. "My father and I helped him find his direction. When Father died, my husband took over the soup kitchen and married me." Her eyes sparkled. "That was seven years ago, and every year just gets better."

Peter exchanged a tender look with Missy, anticipating the start of their future together. By the expression in her eyes, she shared the same thought.

Between the three of them, they managed to convince Florence to stay for one bowl of soup. The room had grown more crowded, but Janine led them to a table at the front. Three small children with curly blond hair sat at the edge of one of the plank seats. Peter recognized the oldest boy as the one who'd interrupted their conversation the first time he'd been to the soup kitchen. The smallest of the children, a girl, lid off the bench and ran to Janine, who lifted her up, and Peter realized these must be her children.

Halfway into their meal, Janine's husband moved to the front of the room to speak. Peter was moved, awed, and shocked upon hearing his new friend's history, though he knew the Frenchman had been a gangster. But he found it difficult to believe this calm man standing before him had conned, deceived, assaulted, and even murdered—and had done it all not to just one but many. His forthright, quiet words held no restraint and touched hearts. Peter noticed Florence reach for her handkerchief to blot her eyes. When their host spoke of his long, difficult journey to find God, she let the tears stream down her face, no longer bothering to stanch their flow. Peter lifted a silent prayer that she would find the peace their host had.

The Frenchman concluded his testimony with an invitation for salvation, and several rough-looking men went toward him and asked for prayer. With head bowed, Florence shook with suppressed sobs but didn't move from the table. Janine sank beside her, wrapping her arm around the flapper's shoulders, saying nothing, only holding her.

Peter swallowed over the emotion of the moment and squeezed Missy's hand. She turned to him, her eyes brimming with tears.

"I need to return to the hotel and check out. Will you be all right here?"

She nodded. "You'll find a telephone and call Aunt Maria? She must be so worried."

"Of course. I'll return shortly." He kissed her cheek.

At the hotel, Peter made quick work of packing his valise and checking out of his room, also collecting his box from the hotel safe. At the front desk, a quick call to Maria reassured the woman, and she agreed that Peter must get Missy out of town with all haste and not bring her home. To his relief, he didn't spot any of Guido's men and wondered if the feared gangster remained unaware of Missy's escape because of the raid. Once he returned to the soup kitchen, he noticed Missy in conversation with Janine and stepped back outside to give the women some time to talk. He strode a short distance away, looking out over the dark ocean.

With no one about, he leaned against one of the wharf's pilings, withdrew the box from his pocket, and stared at it, thinking of his next mission.

"Mon ami, something troubles you?"

Startled, Peter swung around, losing his hold on the box. It fell to the ground, the lid popped off, and the string of diamonds spilled at his feet. His host moved swiftly, before Peter could use his cane to bend over and collect the necklace.

Holding the gems up to his eyes, his host studied the sparkling facets a long moment, then turned to Peter, his expression flabbergasted. "Where did you get this?"

Confused by his demanding tone, Peter held out his hand for the jewels. "I assure you; no foul play was involved. It belongs to my mother. In England."

"Your mother?" He stared at Peter as if he'd struck him. "What is her name?"

"Lady Annabelle Caldwell. Why do you ask?"

It took him a moment to respond, and when he did, his voice was hoarse. "Merely curious." He handed the diamonds back to Peter, searching his face a moment, then picked up the box and offered that, too. "I apologize for startling you. My wife often tells me I am too silent. A word of caution: this area is filled with destitute men. If you do not wish to invite trouble, I advise you to keep that well hidden."

Peter placed the necklace inside the box, pocketing it. His friend was right; he had been foolish to unearth it from his coat. Several feet farther, and it could have ended up in the ocean.

"I came to tell you that you're welcome to stay overnight, though it might be crowded and not as comfortable as you're accustomed to."

"Thank you for your hospitality, but I've already made

arrangements for two rooms at a hotel near Penn Station. Our train leaves in the morning. If you could drive us there, I would be most obliged."

"Of course."

Inside, Peter and Missy said their good-byes.

Florence took Peter aside. "Thank you," she said, her eyes steadier and more sincere than Peter had ever seen them. Her earlier tears had done damage to her powdered face, but he'd never seen it look softer. "No one ever cared enough to grab me like you did and make me come with you. You're quite a guy, a real prince." She grinned. "I hope you and Melissa have a happy life together."

"And you? What of your life?" Since he'd forced Florence to escape with them, he felt somehow responsible for her welfare.

"Janine has offered to shelter me here for a while. You were right; I can't go back. Guido's men know I was the one who helped you spring Melissa."

"And for that you have my undying gratitude." He took her hand and on impulse kissed the back of it, as he would for any lady of noble bearing. "I wish you the very best, Florence."

Flustered, she remained speechless a moment, then shook her head and smiled. "You really *are* a prince."

"And I want to add my thanks for helping Peter find me," Missy said coming up beside him.

Disconcerted, Florence found it hard to look Missy in the eye. "No hard feelings about. . .you know?"

"No hard feelings." Her expression sincere, Missy hugged Florence good-bye.

The drive to the hotel started silently, each of them immersed in their own thoughts.

"Do you think she'll be all right?" Missy finally asked.

"We'll make sure she is," their host assured. "Don't worry. We'll take care of your friend."

Soon they pulled up to the front of the hotel. Once they

climbed out of the vehicle, their host looked at Peter from his rolled-down window.

"You have found much in your quest, *mon ami,* and have learned many things that have given you both joy and pain. Before we part, I want to share with you a piece of advice Janine's father once told me: 'It is not where you come from that's important; rather it is who you are and what you make of yourself.'"

Moved, Peter shook his friend's hand, then realized something extraordinary. "With all that we've been through together, I don't even know your name."

He chuckled. "It's Eric."

"Eric. . . ?"

"Just Eric." He smiled at both of them, tipped his hat to Missy in farewell, and drove away.

nineteen

When Peter first told Missy they would be staying at a children's reformatory, she'd been anxious about what to expect, but Lyons' Refuge was nothing like she'd imagined.

Once they'd taken the train to Ithaca, Stewart and Charleigh Lyons met them at the station. Missy's first thought was that the striking couple—she with her red hair and he with his gray at the temples—were much too kind to be jail wardens, not that she'd ever met any.

Children overran the farm, which seemed more of a country haven than a disciplinary institution. As Missy and Peter exited the car, the smaller ones came running up to see, followed by older boys and girls who approached more slowly, their expressions every bit as curious. Most of the children were darlings—though Missy doubted she would ever remember all their names—and she dreamed of the day she and Peter would have little ones of their own.

Missy soon met the other guiding forces who ran the reformatory: Brent and Darcy Thomas and Bill and Sarah Thomas, each of them remarkable in their own way. As the afternoon wore on, her qualms evaporated and a measure of much-needed peace stole into her heart.

That evening, Charleigh and Darcy, both of them originally from London, dominated Peter, obviously thrilled to have a fellow countryman with whom to discuss the latest news from home. Missy watched a moment, admiring how Peter patiently fielded the women's excited questions. Then, without bringing attention to herself, she slipped outside to the porch.

Though the crisp air chilled her face, the muted softness of the snow on the acres of ground brought with it a calm she hadn't felt in a long time. Above, the moon shone full and bright, bringing with it a tranquility all its own. The door opened, and Missy turned to see who'd joined her.

"It's awfully cold out here," one of the older girls of the refuge noted, a brunette with a vivacious personality. The smattering of light freckles across her nose only added to her appeal.

"Yes, but right now, I like the cold if it means I can look at a view like this. . . .Miranda, right?"

The girl nodded. Missy placed her at sixteen or seventeen.

"Are you one of Darcy's, Charleigh's or Sarah's?"

Miranda laughed. "None of the above, though I think of all three of them as my mothers. But let me help you. The twins, Robert Brent and Beatrice, belong to Darcy and Brent, as do Madeline, Lizzy, Roger, and Matthew. Clemmie, Stewart Jr., and Scottie are Charleigh and Stewart's, and Sarah and Bill are the parents of Josiah, David, Hannah, and Esther. All the rest of the children are reformers like me."

"Reformers?"

"We took a vote a few years ago and decided to call ourselves that. Not only are we being reformed, but also we are the next generation who plan to initiate reforms for the betterment of society. Soon, thanks to Mrs. Lyon's father and his scholarship program, I'll go to college. Once I earn my teaching degree, I'll return to the refuge and give back some of what these wonderful people have given to me."

"And believe you me, that day won't come soon enough!"

Both women jumped as a robust, good-looking young man came around the side of the porch, his arms full of firewood.

"Clint, you shouldn't sneak up on a person like that!" Miranda scolded, though Missy noted the light in her eyes as she watched him take the stairs.

"Who's sneaking?" His smile was wide. "I made about as much noise as humanly possible without calling out to announce myself."

"Where's Joel? I thought he was with you."

"He's packing." Clint looked at Missy. "Joel's one of the oldest boys at the refuge; we're all pretty proud of him. He's enlisted in the army, and we're giving him a sendoff tonight. You guys got here just in time to join the fun."

"That's wonderful." Missy continued to be amazed by those whose lives had been improved by this place. From the little she'd seen, a few of the newer residents experienced difficulties, but most of the older ones seemed mature and emotionally stable.

"Did I hear Darcy mention that you're planning to have your wedding here soon?" Miranda asked.

"Yes, once my aunt arrives. We decided to wait until she can come."

Clint moved in close to the girl. "One day, maybe we'll have our own wedding here, eh, Miranda?"

Pink flames leapt to the girl's cheeks. "Clint, hush! You're incorrigible." She pushed him away, but Missy noticed the slight smile that tilted her lips. "I really need to get back inside and help Clemmie make that sweet bread. She's taking Joel's leaving really hard; she has such a crush on him for being almost ten," she explained to Missy. "I just wanted to make sure you're okay."

"I'm fine." Missy gave a reassuring smile. As the two youngsters retreated inside the house, Missy's mind approached the memory of last night.

Today she *was* fine, but once they'd arrived at the hotel the previous evening and Peter had escorted her to her room, she'd fallen apart.

The aftermath of all she'd experienced hit her hard once they were alone, and she'd been unable to prevent the release from coming. Mortified, she'd buried her face in her hands so Peter wouldn't see her tears.

He had drawn her close and held her long, kissing her hair, whispering warm reassurances of her safety, telling her he would only be in the next room and would keep watch over her. She hadn't wanted him to release her, but when he bid her goodnight, she had regained a semblance of control.

"Hullo, what are you doing out here?"

At the sudden sound of his voice, her heart jumped, and she turned.

Peter closed the door behind him. "Just taking a breath to rest?"

She grinned at his teasing words. "Did you talk things over with Charleigh?"

"I'm waiting until tomorrow for that; the house is abuzz with this farewell party they've planned." He moved to stand beside her, and for an undisturbed moment, they stared at the scenery together. He pulled Mr. Harper's book from his pocket. "There's something in here I think might interest you. I read the remainder of this on the train; you were sleeping, and I didn't want to wake you."

Missy almost felt afraid to take the book, as if by doing so, the past might unfurl and entangle her in its folds. Joining with Peter on his quest to uncover his answers hadn't involved her history; she feared that whatever he wanted her to discover in this book did.

"It's all right. I think you'll find it well worth the effort."

His eyes shone with tenderness, and she took the journal, slipping it into her coat pocket. Then she slipped her arms around his neck and kissed him hard, burying her misgivings in the warmth of his arms.

"Whatever would I do without you, Peter?"

"It's a good thing you'll never have to find out, because like it or not, you're stuck with me."

She grinned. "Oh, I definitely like it," she whispered and kissed him again.

❧

An hour later, everything remained in an uproar. Missy offered her help, and when the women discovered she'd worked in a restaurant for more than half her life, they gratefully put her to work. She helped set the three tables in the big dining room, observing the refuge's inhabitants as she did.

Joel, the guest of honor, was a handsome young man, and from his rakish smile and the comic mischief in his blue eyes, Missy assumed he knew the ladies found him attractive. He reminded Missy of Peter, with the same blue eyes and almost angelic quality to his features, but Joel seemed a little too wild. And from what Missy could tell, Clemmie wasn't the only girl at the refuge infatuated with the fair-haired man and his charismatic charm.

Two girls, reformers both younger than Miranda, helped Missy set the tables. She was surprised the items even made their way to the tablecloth and didn't go crashing to the floor, since the girls couldn't seem to take their eyes off Joel for a moment. He stood by the window, oblivious to their infatuated stares, and spoke with a short, redheaded young man.

Missy giggled, realizing the girls' smitten behavior reflected how she had conducted herself around Peter. No wonder Maria thought she'd lost all sense!

Joel turned to look at her and approached the table. Missy sensed the girl standing nearest her almost drop the plate. Instead, Fran drew it to her chest and held it there.

"Miss Reynolds," Joel addressed her, "since you lived in the Big Apple, perhaps you can settle an argument. Was Arnold Rothstein shot at the Park Central Hotel or at the Waldorf-Astoria? My friend Herbert here insists it was the Waldorf, but I remember reading about it being the Park Central Hotel."

She sensed no spitefulness in his clear eyes, but she tensed at the question. Only those in charge at the refuge knew of her abduction and close escape from gangsters, and she wondered why so many men enjoyed discussing crime and the mobs that terrorized New York. She had overheard many a conversation as she'd waited on tables in her uncle's restaurant.

"It was the Park Central."

"See there!" Joel turned a triumphant smile on his friend. "I knew it."

Herbert grumbled, and Missy's mind revisited past days. Her hand shook, almost knocking a glass over onto the plate. If it had been the Waldorf-Astoria where the mobster Mr. Rothstein had met his demise three weeks earlier, Peter might have been caught as an innocent bystander in the crossfire. She couldn't wait to get out of New York State and put all this behind them.

For a moment, Missy wondered how she would handle ocean travel. The memories of that last night on the *Titanic* had never departed, but to stay in New York? That wasn't an option since Guido had become a real threat, and no longer a distant admirer.

Delectable food soon covered the tables, and good company filled the room. Joel, Herbert, Tommy, Lance, and Clint, the oldest boys at the refuge, linked arms and sang along with the phonograph. They mangled popular tunes such as "S'Wonderful" and "I Wanna Be Loved by You" in an absurd manner, giving everyone a good laugh. Missy thought the five young men should be on vaudeville. Caught up in the merriment of the evening, she recognized other show tunes played, and when Peter asked if she would sing for them, Missy readily agreed.

She looked through the stack of records, finally deciding on a selection to which she knew the words by heart. She handed the record to Clemmie, a pert redhead with intelligent green eyes, who'd taken on the task of changing records.

Missy opened her mouth and sang the first lines of the love song. She couldn't help but notice everyone's frank amazement. At the audience reaction, a twinge of embarrassment tugged at her as it always did, and she turned her attention to Peter, focusing only on him.

The song mirrored Missy's heart, and she sang it from the depths of her soul. She made the words her own as she explained how she'd always scoffed at love before, but the first time she'd glimpsed his blue eyes, the moment his hand clasped hers, her heart had stood still. And from then on, she'd belonged to no other.

After she let the last clear note fade into the air, wild applause burst throughout the room, and a few boys whistled through their fingers. Joel's voice rose above the commotion.

"That was some of the best singing I've ever heard," he enthused, then turned to Herbert. "Was it just me, or did you get the feeling they were the only two people in the room?"

Missy felt a blush color her face at his mischievous teasing but didn't look away from Peter. "We were," she mouthed to him, and he smiled.

twenty

"Mr. Lyons, Mrs. Lyons, are you sure it wouldn't be too great an imposition? Missy and I can easily find a chapel, since we have a license."

"Nonsense, Peter. We've never had a wedding at the refuge; I should love preparing for such an event, and I know Darcy will too." She leaned forward. "And you really must call us Charleigh and Stewart."

He gave a slight nod to the lovely redhead, though he felt odd addressing the older couple in such a manner. Still, they had a way of making him feel comfortable, as if their home were his, and since Charleigh, as well as Darcy, was British, Peter felt a connection to them.

"Tell me, how's your mother?" Charleigh smiled. "I haven't heard from her in years. We only exchanged letters twice, and that was shortly after I married Stewart and we started the refuge. Have you other siblings? She had Gwen and Edward at the time."

"Yes. There are now seven children, actually." Reminded of the real reason he'd sought out Charleigh, he withdrew the box from his pocket. "She sends her best wishes. . . ." He removed the lid and laid the box on the kitchen table in front of her. "And this."

Months ago, when his mother had asked him to deliver the necklace, Peter's curiosity had been piqued. He'd expected a surprised or confused reaction, certainly, but now felt alarmed when every ounce of color drained from Charleigh's face.

"Darling, are you all right?" Stewart left his chair and dropped to his knee beside her, putting his hand to her back.

She picked up the string of diamonds, peering at them more

closely, then dropped the glittering necklace on the table as if it were a snake and might bite her.

"Why would she do this? Why?"

Pain filled her voice, confusing Peter. "It belonged to her mother." He related all he knew. "She put aside other jewelry for the girls to inherit, but she said this particular necklace gave her heartache because it reminded her of the *Titanic* and of losing her father. I never saw her wear it and believe she kept it hidden away all these years. She did say one other thing." He hesitated, hoping his mother's confusing message wouldn't cause further upset. "She mentioned you once sought this for all the wrong reasons, and now she wants to give it to you for the reasons that are good and right."

"Good and right?" Charleigh shook her head, tears brimming in her green eyes. "Whatever does she mean?"

"I cannot say for certain, since she didn't share anything further, but perhaps. . .perhaps she meant for you to sell it and use the money to help you here with your school." Though if that were true, Peter wondered why she hadn't asked Lawrence to invest financially instead.

A dawning look filled Charleigh's eyes. "And perhaps this is Annabelle's way of showing she's completely forgiven me."

"Forgiven you?"

Charleigh nodded. "On the *Titanic*, my associate and I stole this very necklace. The night of the disaster, I took it from his cabin, and weeks later, after I was presumed dead, I returned it to your mother."

Stunned, Peter couldn't respond.

"Peter," Stewart spoke into the silence. "You mentioned you came here early because of your escape from gangsters. For reasons not mine to disclose, I need to ask—did you tell anyone of your destination? Anyone at all?"

With a look of alarm, Charleigh turned to her husband. "Several crime families inhabit Manhattan, Stewart. You don't actually believe it could be Vittorio?. . .Is it?" She addressed her question to Peter.

Recognizing the name of the mobster, Peter felt uneasy. "Not Vittorio, no. But his nephew Guido and his men abducted Missy."

"Oh, my."

Peter didn't understand their reactions, but the news clearly upset them. He rose from his chair. "We don't wish to impose, and evidently we've unknowingly brought trouble to your household. If you can recommend a hotel, I should appreciate it."

"Sit down, Peter." Stewart's voice was grave. "We don't want you to go anywhere. Under the circumstances, perhaps you should know the truth. Excuse me a moment."

Confused, Peter watched him leave the room.

"Don't look so distressed." Charleigh's voice trembled, but kindness filled her eyes. "You and Missy are both welcome here. We wouldn't dream of having you stay anywhere else."

Mildly reassured, Peter nodded.

Soon Stewart returned with both Bill and Brent. In features, the brothers could be twins, but similarities stopped there. Bill's face and arms were bronzed though it was late November, and his hair grew long. Brent reminded Peter of one of his professors, with the precise clothing and manner to match, and it came as no surprise that he taught at the refuge. Where Brent was slender and refined, Bill seemed more a man ready to tackle the outdoors. Peter found it odd how Bill's Polynesian wife, Sarah, was so quiet and elegant, while Brent's fun-loving wife, Darcy, was gregarious to the point of being brash.

Charleigh rose from the table to start a pot of tea. Bill took a seat across from Peter and came straight to the point. "Stewart mentioned you had dealings with someone we're both acquainted with, and he asked me to share some of my history." His expression grim, he clasped his hands on the table in front of him. "Before I met my wife, I used to work for a crime ring run by Vittorio. I was framed for his son's murder and had to flee for my life, but they found me and almost killed my wife. They did kill our unborn child."

Peter stared, bewildered. "You're the second man I've met who once worked for Vittorio—he's the only one I told of our destination," he added to Stewart. "No one else knows except Missy's aunt, and she only knows I took her to an acquaintance of my mother's in Ithaca. If I hadn't felt he was trustworthy, I wouldn't have spoken so freely to him, I assure you."

Stewart drew his brows together. "Who is this man?"

"He runs a soup kitchen, a mission. He's married with children, and his sole purpose in life is helping people and spreading the gospel."

Stewart nodded, seeming relieved.

"You say he worked for Vittorio," Bill said, his manner still just as tense. "How do you know you can trust him?"

After all Bill and his wife had been through, Peter understood the man's caution, and he shared all he knew. "He had a most amazing testimony. He was once a con artist, a mobster, and a murderer, but his prison guard had a habit of speaking the Word along with a desire to save souls. He also told me the woman he'd wronged the most was the one who taught him forgiveness, and if she'd not done that, he might not have listened to the guard. But he did, and it changed his life. While visiting his establishment, I observed a number of people seeking salvation upon hearing his witness and going to him for prayer. I truly don't think you need worry about his motives."

Stewart nodded. "I'm convinced."

"Well, I'm not," Bill insisted. "Didn't he give you his name? Since he worked for Vittorio, I might know him."

"Yes, of course. His name is Eric."

The teakettle crashed to the floor, and the men swung around to look at Charleigh. "Eric?" Her face had gone almost white.

"What was his last name?" Stewart demanded, his manner now as intent as Bill's.

"He didn't give it."

"Eric," Charleigh whispered, grabbing the counter for support and covering her mouth with her other hand.

Stewart hurried to her side to wrap his arm around her. "Charleigh, we don't know for sure it's him."

"Tell me." Charleigh spoke as if she'd not heard him. "Did he speak with a French accent? Is he blond and tall? Dark blue eyes?"

A sense of unreality swept through Peter's confusion. "Yes."

Her eyelids fluttered closed, while Stewart's jaw hardened, and suddenly Peter understood.

"You were the woman he wronged, the one who forgave him." Charleigh gave a stiff nod.

"And your friend who showed him an act of kindness?"

"What?"

Peter explained, and she moved to sit down. "Darcy gave him money to buy a coat. He was sick and didn't have one. It was snowing." She spoke in a monotone.

Dumbfounded, Peter stared at the table, and his mind clicked the scattered pieces together. "Now it makes sense. Both of you reacted with the same shock upon seeing the necklace. He was your accomplice, the one on the *Titanic*." Peter wondered why Eric hadn't shared with him that he, too, was on the ship.

"Eric saw the necklace?" Horrified confusion filled her voice. "And he knew you were bringing it here?"

"Yes." Their anxiety caused him doubt. "He told me if I didn't want to invite danger from destitute men, I should keep it well hidden."

Charleigh gave a humorless laugh. "He should know."

"We've only one way to learn the truth," Stewart said with grim determination. "Can you find this soup kitchen? Will you take us to him?"

"What of Missy?" Peter stalled. "I can't leave her here alone, and I certainly can't take her back to Manhattan."

"She'll be fine. Brent and Bill will be here, as well as the older boys. Besides, if the man we know as Eric is the one whom you told of your destination, he would tell no one else, especially if his desire is to get the necklace. . .or to gain revenge."

Peter desperately tried to follow the conversation. "Revenge? For what?"

Charleigh had recovered, but her smile was grim. "For losing what he had—me and the necklace. And for us putting him in prison."

❧

Missy frowned, shaking her head. "I don't want you to go back there without me. I could wear a wig; no one would recognize me."

"No, Missy." Frustrated, Peter pushed a hand through his hair, stepping away from her.

She followed. "You promised you would never leave me, that we would stick together. We're a team, remember?" She knew she was being unreasonable but couldn't help herself. She didn't want to be separated from Peter again and couldn't quell the fear that it might be permanent this time.

"We are a team, yes." He dropped his cane and placed his hands on either side of her head, tilting her face up, his eyes intense as he looked into hers. "But I would never forgive myself if something happened to you, if one of Guido's informers should somehow see you and report to him. I love you, Missy. I'd give my life for you, and I refuse to put you in a potentially dangerous situation."

She felt her heart melt. "I love you too, Peter. It's only because I love you so much that I want to go with you." She sensed him begin to tense again and added, "But I'll stay. I need to do a few things before the wedding, so I suppose it is best." She searched for something positive to say. "I can't believe Aunt Maria is finally coming, though five days seems like forever. I know she's had to be careful not to give our location away on the chance she's followed, but this waiting's been hard."

"For me, too." He touched his lips to hers in a light kiss. "I'll be back tonight, I promise."

"I'll hold you to that. But I *am* going along with Brent and Darcy to drive you to the station."

"About that. . ."

She gathered her brows, sensing she wouldn't like what was coming.

"Charleigh's decided she's going too, though Stewart is none too happy about it. I'm afraid there won't be room in the car now since Bill is also going. He and Eric were friends, only he knew him as Philip, and oddly enough, they both saved each other's lives," Peter explained.

Sidetracked for a moment within this odd triangle in which they'd found themselves, Missy shook her head. "It's all so strange, isn't it? I, for one, don't believe there's a cruel bone in Eric's body; he was so kind to us and so sincere with those who prayed with him."

"I agree. But after all the Lyons have been through regarding him, I suppose they feel they must do this to put their minds at rest."

Missy smiled, and Peter's expression grew curious.

"What?"

"I was just thinking: it all goes back to that message—how sometimes God waits for His perfect timing to bring things to pass so that many can be blessed and not just a few. Perhaps in your quest, He used you as the catalyst to bring about something more important than you ever dreamed."

He looked at her in awe. "Missy, you're an amazing woman. I never thought of that, but I think you're right."

An hour later, once Peter left with the others for the station, Missy grew discouraged. Later when Darcy and her husband returned, Darcy noticed Missy standing at the window in the parlor and slipped her arm around her.

"Aw, cheer up, luv. He'll be back tonight. Won't he, Brent?"

"I've been given instructions as to the precise time of their return."

Missy smiled, trying to appear brave. "It's just hard to be apart, even for a day."

"Ah, young love," Darcy said on a sigh. "How well I remember."

Brent smiled at his wife. "And it only improves with age."

"It does at that, guv'ner. It does at that!"

Darcy laughed, and Missy looked on with a smile. They were still so much in love, and watching them gave her hope. Marriage wasn't easy; she'd learned that by witnessing her mother's failures. But Missy *would* succeed because she fervently wanted a life with Peter. She would work hard to be the wife he needed.

Missy excused herself and went upstairs to the room she'd been given. Closing her eyes, she sank to her bed and drew the comforter around herself, trying to crowd out the chills of fear.

As a child, whenever someone had left her for a time, she had grown anxious they might not return. She recalled those few days Peter had been absent from her life because he'd been ill. At the time, her insecurities had caused her to doubt that he would return. And though she felt confident in his love now, niggling questions persisted, despite her best efforts to quell them.

From the moment they'd met, she had brought Peter physical pain, and later she'd only added to his emotional anguish. Guido's men almost killed him because of her! She wouldn't blame Peter if he changed his mind and never came back, but her heart entreated his return.

"Dear Lord, I need to learn to trust. Help me. I don't know how, and I desperately want to. You gave Peter guidance; help me to trust."

A calm drifted into her spirit as she focused on His strength, which seemed to enfold and comfort her. She grew so relaxed that she stretched out on the bed and fell asleep.

When she awoke, Mr. Harper's journal was the first thing she saw. A current of guilt jetted through her.

She had promised to read the journal but had put the book aside and concentrated on other matters concerning Peter and their upcoming wedding. Now with him gone, she had no more excuses.

Missy picked up the book from the bedside table, stared at it a long moment, then opened the frayed cover. As she struggled through the first pages, she noticed little order to the entries. They meandered here and there and would often leave off, commence with the introduction of a new person, then reintroduce an older subject pages later.

Her earlier trepidation led to amusement as she tried to follow the ambiguous scribblings of a writer. Far into the book, she found what she'd nervously anticipated:

> *Doña Ortega—Scandinavian blond, blue eyes, full-figured, mid-20s; traveling alone with small daughter and maid. Reserved to the extreme of being snobbish, therefore fitting in quite well with all other matrons of whom I've made acquaintance; I sense pain in her eyes—involving her ill-behaved daughter? Her missing husband? Seating arrangements have placed us at same table throughout voyage; perhaps I will learn answers then.*

Ill-behaved? Missy frowned. The following paragraph introduced yet another passenger. Intrigued despite her desire to resist, Missy flipped a few pages until she found more:

> *Doña Ortega—has habit of pressing three fingers to her temple when upset. Is upset often. Daughter—Missy—spitting image of mother. I sense tension between them but cannot place cause for it. Perhaps my earlier assessment of child was unfair; if I had belonged to such a mother, I might also have made myself scarce by habitually running away. Child carries doll everywhere, went so far as to ask steward for chair to place doll in. Her comment brought laughter from all those*

at our table, all except her mother. The manner in which the doña narrows eyes at doll—perhaps not a gift from her?

Missy's eyes widened as she relived her childhood through an adult passenger's eyes. She flipped through several pages until she found more:

I was put in a most awkward position today after having fallen asleep in chair against alcove wall in reading room. I awoke to hear voices. On other side of wall in adjoining alcove, the doña spoke with Mrs. J. J. Brown (who could mistake that strong voice?). Am amazed Mrs. Brown able to crack through the doña's icy exterior but have found her to be an amazing woman. Felt some shame for not making my presence known by clearing my throat. Instead, I remained quiet and eavesdropped. Soon, I determined the conversation was brought on by the disastrous outcome of a birthday party the doña had planned for her daughter, after which Missy made herself scarce by running away to hide. She is quite adept at this.

Doña Ortega—a very insecure woman (*note: would make good character type for planned novel, perhaps one of the sisters?). She's certain husband will take daughter away; claims he seeks Missy's love with his gifts, including doll. The peculiar thing is child and the don are not blood-related, so why such fears? The doña admitted she's a poor excuse for a mother (few could disagree) and Missy would do better with anyone else, and I quote, "I'm afraid to keep her, and I'm afraid to lose her. In my own way, I love her, but I don't think that love will ever equal what she needs." One can only pity a creature like that.

In shock, Missy stared at the page until it blurred. Mother had told a passing stranger that she loved Missy but, for whatever reason, had neglected to tell Missy the same. Faced with the truth of her mother's insecurities, Missy could only wonder. She'd never thought of the statuesque Doña

Ortega as being anything other than a strong, cold woman, a former prima donna who asserted complete control of every situation. To find out otherwise brought a trickle of compassion, a feeling she'd never felt toward her mother. Like Missy, the doña had struggled with personal doubts and fears, and that made Missy not only begin to understand her mother a little better but also feel connected to her in a way she never had been before.

twenty-one

Eric exited the soup kitchen door, his expression calm and not the least bit surprised. His next words proved it.

"I thought you might come. You're looking well, Charleigh."

Charleigh gave a barely discernable nod. She searched his face, as if trying to associate it with the memory from her past, then turned her shocked gaze to his four-year-old daughter clasped at his side. From big blue eyes, Lynette observed the newcomers with shy interest while keeping her arms firmly fastened around her father's neck.

"Bill, it's good to see you again." Eric stuck out his hand, and Bill shook it.

"You, too, Phil, er. . .Eric. I want to thank you for the warning you sent years ago. About Vittorio."

Eric nodded. "Of course."

Peter had a difficult time trying to determine Charleigh's feelings, but Stewart's blazing eyes and clenched mouth told all.

"If this is what you're after," Stewart said, pulling the diamond necklace from his pocket and shoving it in Eric's face, "take it! It will save you coming to the refuge to torment our women and children again." The little girl's eyes widened as she stared at the jewels sparking glimmers of colored fire in the morning sunlight.

Eric sighed. "I don't want your necklace."

"Then what *do* you want?"

Eric didn't answer right away. He kissed Lynette's temple, set her down on the ground, and told her in French to go to her mother. Once she'd scampered off, he regarded them gravely.

"I want peace among us, and since you ask, Stewart, I want your forgiveness."

"Forgiveness?" Stewart's contained rage altered into open disbelief. "After all that's happened—after you broke into our home and held a gun on my wife—you expect me to *forgive* you?"

"*Non*, I do not expect it. I humbly ask for it. Whether you choose to give forgiveness or not is your decision alone." When Stewart gave no answer and all four of them continued to stare, Eric motioned to the building behind him. "Please, let us leave the street and continue this discussion inside."

Peter hesitated. "I'll have to decline. We're here for only a few hours, and I must attend to other matters. How is Florence?"

Eric smiled. "She is doing much better, *mon ami*. She helps Janine with the children while Janine serves our guests."

Peter nodded, satisfied.

Bill turned Peter's way. "Would you like some company?"

Although surprised, Peter sensed Bill felt what he did, that Eric and the Lyons needed time alone to talk. "That would be splendid. I want to visit the restaurant and collect Missy's things." He also wanted to find out what had occurred since their escape and if Missy remained in danger from Guido or if the man had been thrown into jail after the raid.

An hour later, his worst fear was realized.

"Guido wasn't at the speakeasy when the raid took place," Tony said while Maria went to Missy's room to gather her things into a trunk. "Two of his men came to question me about Missy; they watched the restaurant for three days but caused no trouble and have not been here since." He looked around the almost empty restaurant and leaned in closer. "I hear my customers talk. One of them is a fed, Moe Smith, who brought with him his partner, Izzy." He shook his head. "They wear bizarre disguises to sneak into suspected speakeasies, and that night from what I hear, Moe wore a dress."

"Really?" Peter raised his brows in incredulous amusement. He remembered the strange couple who'd entered the speakeasy before he'd found Missy. The ugly woman in the fur coat had looked more like a man with dark bushy brows and a strong jaw, and the companion had also seemed out of place with his long beard. He wondered if they had been the two agents.

"An anonymous call led them to a speakeasy; I heard him say the tipster revealed that Guido had kidnapped a woman, and I know this must be our Missy."

Peter straightened in his chair, alert. He had told only one man about his plan to go there and rescue Missy. "Eric," he mouthed to Bill across the table. Eric's ex-associate smiled and nodded.

Once Maria returned to the table, Peter regarded her warmly. "I'm relieved to know your family is well. Now, I have a favor to ask, something to which I hope you'll both be agreeable."

❧

Missy could barely sit still as she glanced at the mantel clock for what must be the fifth time in as many minutes. The train should have arrived thirty-five minutes ago; what was taking so long?

At last, the whir of a car's engine sounded, and she raced for the door, ready to throw herself into Peter's embrace. She stopped short when the door opened and a familiar, dark-haired woman exited the vehicle.

"Aunt Maria!" She ran to Maria's open arms and hugged her. "Everyone's all right?" Missy pulled away. "Tony? The children?" At Maria's nod, Missy exhaled in relief. "But how—you said you were coming on Saturday."

"Peter thought you might not wish to delay the wedding any longer than you have already." Maria's eyes sparkled with joy. "I have brought your trunk with all your things."

"Herbert, you and Clint take the trunk to Missy's room, please," Missy heard Brent instruct behind her.

Missy turned her attention toward the car as Peter exited.

His gaze seemed both affectionate and uncertain. "I hope you don't mind."

"Mind?" She laughed and rushed forward to hug him, not caring what anyone thought. "You mad, impulsive Englishman! Why should I mind? It's what I've wanted all along."

"Actually," he whispered, for her ears alone, "I didn't just do it for you; it's what I wanted as well."

"Oh, this is smashing!" Charleigh trilled. Missy noted that her face seemed to glow with a peace she'd not seen before and assumed all had gone well with Eric. Before she could ask about their trip, Charleigh moved toward the stairs. "I'll ring the minister and see if he's free tomorrow."

"I can't wait to see Darcy's face when we ask her to bake a wedding cake tonight," Stewart said, and he, too, seemed more relaxed than Missy had ever seen him. Peace replaced the former lines of stress on his face, and his eyes sparkled with exuberance.

"Oh, please, no," Missy said, keeping one arm around Peter. "Under the circumstances, I don't need a cake."

"Are you kidding?" Bill smiled at her. "My sister-in-law looks for every excuse invented to bake. She won't mind a bit, I'm sure." Sarah came out onto the porch, and Bill hurried toward her, and she to him. The two embraced as if they'd been apart for weeks and not one day. Oblivious to everyone but each other, they tenderly kissed.

Missy smiled. "It will be like that for us, too, I know it."

"I have no doubt in my mind," Peter said with a grin. Two of Bill and Sarah's children came running out the door, squealing as they ran to embrace their father. With the focus on the Thomas family, Missy moved closer to Peter and kissed him, hardly daring to believe that tomorrow this wonderful man would be her husband.

twenty-two

Peter donned his best clothes, knowing that in less than an hour, his sweet Missy would become his wife. Taking this moment of solitude to collect his thoughts, he moved to the bedroom window and stared out over the distant treetops.

He felt no compunction whatsoever at the idea of taking Missy as his bride and sharing a life with her. But Guido still lurked out there, and though Stewart had reassured him they remained safe at the refuge, Peter wouldn't breathe easy until they were well away from New York. Still, God had guided him this far; that much was apparent. And Peter knew He wouldn't abandon them now. Peter thought back to the previous day.

When he'd returned with Bill to the soup kitchen, they'd both been amazed to see Eric and Janine sitting at a table with the Lyons and having a friendly chat. Peter had pulled Eric aside. "You were the tipster who called the feds about the raid, weren't you?"

Eric released a short breath of amusement, then gave a magnanimous shrug. "I figured you could use a little help. Was I wrong?"

"No." Peter chuckled in disbelief, shaking his head. "Why didn't you tell me you were on the *Titanic?*"

"Ah, *mon ami.* That is a time in my life I wish to forget. When I realized you were Annabelle's son. . ." He shook his head in remembered bewilderment. "I felt doubly gratified to know I had given you my assistance."

"And I thank you for all your help."

Eric gave a short nod. "You, too, have helped me. Through your quest to find your family, God has brought reconciliation to all of us." He looked toward Charleigh and Stewart, who were in deep discussion with Janine.

"And I *have* found a family here." Peter thought of all those who'd offered him support these past weeks. "More of a family than I ever dreamed possible."

Still amazed at how God had used his quest to help his new friends breach a wall that spanned almost two decades of pain, remorse, and fear, Peter recalled how Stewart had shaken Eric's hand in good-bye. Charleigh had hugged Janine and then tentatively did the same with Eric, wishing them both well. From that moment on, Peter had sensed a difference in the Lyons, as if they'd found a long-sought peace and had finally embraced freedom.

A knock at the door broke him from his thoughts.

Peter opened it to one of the reformers, a young man named Tommy. They shared one similarity, drawing Peter to the boy who was only a few years younger than he. Tommy had a clubfoot and often seemed unsure of his place in the world.

"Mr. Thomas sent me up to ask if you needed anything," he explained.

Peter regarded him. "Now that I think about it, I do need something. How would you like to be my best man, Tommy?"

The boy's eyes widened. "You mean it?"

"Of course. Missy has asked Stewart to walk her down the aisle, and I could use someone to stand beside me."

"Sure, I'll do it." Tommy's eyes lit up. "That would be swell. So you guys are traveling south along the coast?"

"Yes. To Florida, actually. I decided it would be best to leave New York for the months we must wait before we sail for England."

"I envy you. Any week now, the blizzards should start, and you don't want to be in upstate New York in the dead of winter."

He gave a mock shiver, and Peter laughed, clapping him on the shoulder. "Are you ready to go downstairs?"

"I'm the one who should be asking you that. You're really not a bit nervous, are you? I knew one other guy who married—

Samuel, one of the original reformers—and he was as nervous as a barnyard cat perched on a fence and staring down a pack of hungry dogs."

"Really?" Peter chuckled. "I suppose when a man finds treasure, as I have, he's eager to claim it."

"Yeah, I guess. I wish I'd find a treasure of my own some day."

"You will." Peter gave an encouraging smile.

"Aren't you even the slightest bit uneasy about married life?"

Peter turned the question over in his mind, then smiled. "I learned something these past months, Tommy. With God's guidance in our lives, we're destined to succeed."

❧

"Aunt Maria, it's so beautiful." Awed, Missy smoothed her hand over the creamy white lace of the Spanish-styled wedding gown she wore.

"I took the dress in quite a bit, but I think it fits well."

"It's perfect." Missy turned to hug her aunt. "Thank you for allowing me the honor of wearing your wedding gown."

"Missy, it pleases me so much to do this. You have always been like a daughter to me."

Her words brought with them the memory of her mother, and Missy sobered.

"*Mi niña*, she does love you." Maria correctly guessed Missy's thoughts. The previous evening, unable to sleep from excitement, Missy had spent hours talking with Maria about what she'd found in the journal and about the past. "She just does not know how to express that love."

Missy pondered her aunt's words, coming to a decision. "Do you know where she is now?"

"Up until three years ago, I did. I read in the newspaper that she joined an opera company and was touring with them."

Missy turned to examine her dress in the mirror and fluffed the flounces of the skirt. "If she contacts you, will you let me know? I—I think I would like to write her."

The admission made Maria gasp; for years, Missy had

refused even to speak of her mother. But now. . .now it was time to let go. She didn't want to enter her new life with Peter burdened by bitterness from her past.

Maria's eyes filled with tears. "*Sí,* I will write you."

"And you must come visit us, too." Missy grinned. "I can't wait to see my first castle!"

In three days, she and Peter would take the train to Florida, and later, they would set sail for England. But first. . .Missy took a deep breath, focusing on the present, and nodded to Maria. "I'm ready now."

Ten minutes later, she glided into the white and pink be-ribboned parlor on Stewart's arm in rhythm with a melodious tune playing on the phonograph. Missy's gaze locked with Peter's dazed one the entire time she moved to take her place beside him before the minister.

Gazing into Peter's blue eyes, she found herself. Taking his hand, she came to life, and in anticipating their future together. . .her heart stood still.

epilogue

One year later

"Who would've ever believed that the baby blanket you gave me as a birthday present for my doll seventeen years ago would one day swaddle your first grandchild?" Missy spoke softly, gazing upon the sleeping infant in her arms with all the love a mother could possibly bear. She looked up at her mother-in-law and noted the tears filming her green eyes.

The years had been kind to the Countess, Lady Annabelle Caldwell, bringing with them a distinct softness to her features and a slight silvering to her dark hair. During the past year in which Missy had lived in England with Peter in one wing of the Caldwells' sprawling manor, Missy had resumed her acquaintance with the woman who'd once been so kind to her on a ship full of strangers. She felt blessed to regard Annabelle not only as her mother-in-law but also as a dear friend.

"I cannot believe the blanket is still in such good condition," Annabelle murmured, fingering its snow-white folds.

"Once I quit playing with dolls, I put it away to keep it safe." Missy laughed softly so as not to wake her sleeping son. "Aunt Maria put into that trunk every item I possessed, and I'm glad now she did." She thought about her aunt's most recent letter and was thankful Guido hadn't terrorized the family upon his failure to locate Missy, apparently accepting Tony's explanation that she'd run away.

"Including the dolls I've seen on the bureau in your bedroom?" Annabelle teased, breaking into her thoughts.

Warmth flushed Missy's cheeks, and she grinned. "One day I'll give them to my daughters, especially the doll called Annabelle.

She was my most treasured possession at that time because she reminded me of you."

The countess laid her hand on Missy's shoulder. "I know I've told you this often, but I thank God every day for bringing you into Peter's life, and I pray you both will be as happy as Lawrence and I have been. To think that the small sassy girl I knew on the *Titanic* is now a member of my family." She shook her head. "I am continually amazed by the way God works things out and brings people together."

"Sassy?" Missy's brows sailed upward.

Annabelle laughed. "Yes, sassy. But loveable and sweet, too."

"Missy?" Gwen stood in the nursery door. Of all her sisters- and brothers-in-law, Missy felt closest to the sixteen-year-old girl. The eldest of the children born after Annabelle and Lawrence had adopted Peter, Gwen possessed striking looks and a quiet manner. "Peter asked me to tell you he's ready for you."

"Thank you." Missy placed a kiss on her son's forehead, then carefully transferred him to his grandmother's waiting arms. Still, she hesitated, wondering if he might soon wake up hungry.

"Go on. Clayton will be fine. And be certain not to overtire yourself, dear."

"I won't." Missy looked back one last time to see the charming picture of Annabelle smiling tenderly at her grandson.

On the way downstairs, she met her father-in-law coming up. The earl's thick hair was heavily sprinkled with silver, but despite his years, he retained his trim, strong build. Nor had age diminished his height. He towered almost a foot above Missy. His ice-blue eyes were striking in his distinguished face, and from the day she'd met him, Missy had found Lord Caldwell to be as wonderful as Peter had claimed. Both he and Annabelle had welcomed her into their family as if she'd always belonged there.

"Are you feeling well?" he asked.

Kentucky
CHANCES

3 stories in 1

There independent Kentucky women, three adventurous California men. Whether it's Lovejoy protecting her sister, Daisy protecting her son, or Hattie settling on the belief that there's nothing left to be found in life, the last thing these three women are looking for is love.

Historical, paperback, 352 pages, 5³⁄₁₆" x 8 "

———————————————————

HEARTSONG
PRESENTS

If you love Christian romance...

$10.⁹⁹

You'll love Heartsong Presents' inspiring and faith-filled romances by today's very best Christian authors. . .DiAnn Mills, Wanda E. Brunstetter, and Yvonne Lehman, to mention a few!

When you join Heartsong Presents, you'll enjoy four brand-new, mass market, 176-page books—two contemporary and two historical—that will build you up in your faith when you discover God's role in every relationship you read about!

Imagine. . .four new romances every four weeks—with men and women like you who long to meet the one God has chosen as the love of their lives...all for the low price of $10.99 postpaid.

To join, simply visit www.heartsong presents.com or complete the coupon below and mail it to the address provided.

Mass Market 176 Pages

✂ -